CW00516859

FIGHT LIKE A MAN

THE SHTF SERIES, BOOK ONE

L.L. AKERS

SCORCHED EARTH PUBLISHING, LLC

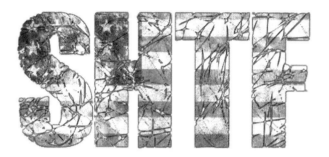

To my prepping partner.
When the poop hits the fan, I'll be your huckleberry.

"**Hello Darkness,** my old friend
I've come to talk with you again
Because a vision softly creeping
Left its seeds while I was sleeping
And the vision that was planted in my brain
Still remains
Within the sound of silence..."
~ Simon & Garfunkel

FOREWORD

As warned by scientists, the Department of defense—and even the 2017 United States presidential candidates—Ted Koppel and countless others, the world as we know it *is* going dark. It's not a matter of *if*, but *when*. It could be terrorists and/or foreign enemies inflicting a cyber-attack by hacking into our systems, or an EMP/nuclear weapon, or even a natural, but unexpected, solar flare.

The lights *are* going out.

It *is* a 'coming, one way or the other.

When it does, the real fear will be that of the predatory darkness found *within* our fellow human beings. There will be no power. No water. No fuel. No readily available food source. Limited medical services. Possibly no transportation. Communications will go down. Systems will catastrophically fail.

Society will collapse.

Until America recovers, police officers, military personnel, firefighters, and other emergency service personnel will have to make a choice between doing their appointed duties—of which they may not be paid—or protecting their own families. Which would *you* choose?

We all know the answer to that. And without proper ongoing services, there *will* be predators. These animals—humans, in fact—will prey on the weak, the unprotected, and the unprepared. Previous friends, neighbors, and business acquaintances too will turn on you when they're desperate. The bad people *will* come. They will come in force, and they will dominate the masses. This apocalyptic event won't discriminate. It doesn't matter whether you're rich or poor; black or white; male or female. You and yours *will* be affected.

I hope you're prepared.

PROLOGUE

THREE MONTHS AFTER THE EVENT

GRAYSON DROPPED into a squat and glared at the mound of freshly turned dirt. He tossed one lone magnolia flower onto the grave; she had loved that sweet scent. He stood to pace back and forth between the two rows of hand-made wooden crosses—already leaning and showing wear and tear from the weather—but still standing guard like tired soldiers over those he had tried to protect.

He'd failed.

He looked over his shoulder. No one else was coming?

Piss poor excuse for a funeral.

He kicked a rock, sending it flying into the air, where it pinged against the small cross on the one shortened grave at the end of the row. His lips tightened as his throat knotted up. His eyes were wet. He swiped at them with the back of his hand.

Grayson hadn't asked for this; to be a leader...to be in charge. He'd married Olivia for a wife and got a family; that part he didn't regret. But the pressure of taking care of Olivia and her sisters, Gabby and Emma, *and* everyone else was too much. This wasn't some fictional story, where the reluctant hero finally steps up to accept his place. He didn't want to be in charge anymore. He *wasn't* a hero; far from it. He wasn't a soldier, either. None of them were. He was just a guy. A middle-aged man with a wife and kid who only wanted them all to be able to live in peace with full bellies and a good night's sleep every night, safe in their beds without fear.

They shouldn't have to fight for every morsel or sip; every breath of air. Every minute of rest. How had it all gone so bad, so quick? Where was the real help from the government? Couldn't *any* of those ABC agencies do something for the American people?

America just had to go sticking their nose in where it didn't belong. *Or did it?* At this point, he didn't even know who their adversary was. Who had attacked the United States with a blow so quiet and deadly that they didn't even need to put boots on the ground?

North Korea was the most likely suspect, but they couldn't have done this. Not alone. Who was the Judas? Russia? China? Which had the most to gain by crippling America? Who had turned on them?

Someone had.

And whoever was responsible was the master of surprise.

They'd never seen it coming. While America was scrambling to point military reinforcements to foreign lands, they'd left their own back yard wide open for a blow that had hobbled the country.

It was over before it began.

Over without the enemy shedding a single drop of blood.

This wasn't even a war; it was a massacre, fought in a flash with no flesh and blood foe invading their lands. No fair fight. Their enemy had struck fast and furious at America using no guns or nukes at all. So much for *fire and fury*, as the president had promised.

As far as he knew, there *was* no fight. This battle hadn't been fought with bullets and bombs.

The only guns being used were against each other in a fight for survival.

So where *were* the *real* soldiers?

He needed help. They all needed help.

In the meantime, how to take care of his family? They shouldn't *have* to suffer. They weren't like the horde of sheeple who'd spent their lives never preparing, thinking something like this could never happen here. Those people had thought the United States was a super power that couldn't ever be taken down.

But he *had* thought it—or something like it—could happen. And he *had* prepared. As had his family. They'd ignored the jabs and rolling eyes of their friends when they'd tried to bring up 'prepping' to warn others. They'd been laughed at and ridiculed. Made to look crazy. But they'd done it anyway.

They'd worn the silly 'prepper' moniker despite the ridicule.

They'd stocked up with bullets, beans, and Band-Aids; and a thousand other things.

But it hadn't been enough.

It was a hard lesson, but he'd learned you cannot prepare for everything.

A sadness washed over him as he stared at the small grave. How many more would there be?

Now that clean water was limited, people were thirsty, dehydrated, and desperate, which made them stupid and *lazy*. They wouldn't always take the time to do what was necessary to make the water safe, and now those same people were paying their dues in sickness, diarrhea and sometimes a never-ending nap. But that wasn't the only thing killing them.

Food was also in high demand.

His stomach growled thinking of the meager supper of rice and beans he'd been lucky to eat today. Who knew what tomorrow would—or wouldn't—bring.

To add to the death toll, bloodthirsty men—fellow Americans—with no conscious or morals had stepped out of the dark to take over, forcibly stealing anything and everything they wanted: food, gas, water, medication, and even *women*.

The real war was now being raged amongst themselves.

If these men took from you, the only way to get it back was to *pay,* and the price was exorbitant. The only currencies good in this day and time were ammo, liquor, drugs, cigarettes, gas and flesh.

Or blood.

Grayson stood and closed his eyes, taking a deep breath. He shook off his sorrow and grit his teeth against the pain, pulling up the anger he'd tried so hard to keep tapped back. He'd had his pity party. Today marked the loss of one too many.

To hell with it.

He was done paying.

1

THE SOUND of silence spread over Grayson like a heavy blanket, nudging him awake.

All was quiet—too quiet. The first peek of sunrise squinted through the blinds, but the room was still dark enough to sleep for a while longer. He rolled over to put his arm around Olivia, expecting to find his wife still snuggled in beside him.

Instead, his hand brushed hair, where there *shouldn't* have been hair. Lots of it. And not silky soft like his wife's.

Coarse and dirty-feeling hair.

He jerked his hand back, but not before waking Ozzie. Too late, he attempted to cover his face for the attack he knew was coming.

Damn dog.

Ozzie was on him in a flash, licking his face to beg for breakfast.

"Get down, Ozzie!"

The dog whined.

"No, it's not time. It's too early."

Grayson rolled over, giving him his back. He'd lay still a few minutes more, remembering that Olivia was gone on a trip to the beach with her sisters—and he was stuck home with her dog.

He sighed. He wasn't looking forward to getting up to no wife again. Although he'd never admit it to Olivia, *no wife* meant *no life* for him.

He'd been in a funk since she'd been gone. Not only did he have a toothache and had to face the dentist later today, but he was dragging ass, feeling lazy and grouchy in general since Olivia had left. It wasn't that he didn't have projects he could do. And she'd left him her own honey-do list in case he got bored. He'd gruffly accepted it and shoved it into a pocket, acting as though he didn't need it. He'd had plenty to do. Didn't want her worrying about him.

Truth was, he'd finished the honey-do list the first day she was gone. And he'd been moping around since then. He'd bribed Ozzie into hanging out with him on the couch, binge-watching Netflix with cold beer and hot chili—and beef jerky and chips for the mutt; dog-farts be damned.

She'd be pissed if she knew he wasn't taking care of himself—or Ozzie—and keeping busy.

His stomach rumbled thinking of all the good food he wasn't eating. While he did most of the cooking for them, Olivia usually took care of breakfast. With her gone, he'd been getting his coffee and breakfast-sandwich from the local service station. He hadn't felt like cooking for only himself. His stomach rumbled again and he vowed to get up and cook real food today. Maybe some bacon biscuits. Definitely coffee. No more canned food and junk.

But first, just one more hour of sleep.

He closed his eyes and lay still, trying to recapture his slumber, when he realized it was too quiet. That had to be what had awoken him.

The sound of silence.

What happened to the fan? He was sure it'd been on when he'd gone to bed last night. It irked him that he'd become such a creature of habit that he couldn't sleep well without the low murmur of the white noise.

He crawled out of the bed and stumbled to the dresser. He turned the knob of the fan to the right, and then to the left.

Nothing.

Maybe it got unplugged somehow, he thought. *Probably the dog...*

He flicked on the lamp to give him some light.

Nothing.

What the—

He looked for the familiar green glow of the alarm clock. It should be beside the fan. Olivia kept moving it away from the bed because he had a tendency to slap the snooze button too much. It annoyed her to hear the alarm go off every seven minutes for an hour.

She gets annoyed too easy.

In the dim light, he found the clock and picked it up. No glowing numbers. It was off. He didn't even know there was a way to turn it *off*. He'd never seen it not lit up before, unless it was unplugged. He pressed the buttons on the top, not sure of what he was pressing. He ran his hand down the power cord all the way to the wall. It was plugged in.

Power must be out.

Now he'd have to get up and find out how long it was going to be out for. It couldn't be a weather thing; the weather in the Carolinas had been beautiful this May. Either the power company was screwing around updating this or that, or someone had hit a pole, knocking out a transformer.

Too bad he was too far from his nearest neighbor to see if their power was out too. Crossing to the window, he raised the blinds to let in as much light as possible and picked up his cell phone to call it in to the power company; maybe if he called early enough, he'd get higher up on the list.

The cell phone lit up and he sighed in relief. He scrolled through his contacts, finding the number for the power company and dialed.

It didn't ring.

No service.

Odd.

A scary thought slid into his mind and he pushed it back out. *Can't be. No way.*

He hurried out of the bedroom, stalking through the house. Every room...no power. No little glowing lights on the TV system. No time showing on the microwave or stove. No hum of a refrigerator. *Nothing.*

He waved off his silly thoughts. Plenty of times that cell phone had failed him. Phone service was spotty at best way out here in the country.

He'd just use the iPad—or PooPad, as Olivia called it, since he took it with him to the bathroom every morning to read the news.

Time management, he'd told her a thousand times.

Sometimes it was easier to get online than it was to make a call. At least that's what Olivia had always said. She was able to get on the internet with that new-fangled 3G or 4G or something, even when they had no power; as long as the tablet was charged.

The power company had an online-reporting site where he could be sure to get on the list for repair service, or maybe see if any news was posted as to why it was out.

Returning to the living room where he'd left the iPad, he told Ozzie to back off, he'd feed him in a minute. The dog was literally right on his heels. With the heavy curtains pulled closed, Grayson could barely see. The coffee table creeped up on him and he stubbed his toe.

The little one.

"Stupid *son* of a—" he screamed, sending Ozzie scurrying away in fright.

Forget it. That shit hurt like hell, but swarping and cussing didn't have the same affect when he was alone; it wouldn't make his toe feel better at all, and it just scared the dog. He hated doing that. Ozzie was his only company; he didn't want him to be afraid. He clenched his teeth against the throbbing, and blew out his breath through his nose.

He'd be glad when Olivia came home.

"It's alright, boy," he said as he hopped the few steps to the couch, flopped down and grabbed the iPad from the coffee table. Ozzie returned, wagging his tail, always quick to forgive. He gave him a quick pat on the head and jabbed a finger on the home button of the iPad, expecting to feel silly when it lit up.

He was right.

It lit right up.

He sighed in relief.

Tapping the internet icon, his mind wandered. How long had the power been out? He'd gone to bed early so in all reality, it could've been off all night. He'd need to check to be sure their food wasn't unthawed or warm. No telling how long it would be before the power company got to him, he might not have power all day and night.

He jumped up, and hurried to the kitchen and opened the freezer door.

An unspoken swear word exploded in his mind.

His penny was sitting in the bottom of a glass of water. A trick he'd learned a long time ago was to fill up a glass of water and freeze it, and then lay a penny atop the ice. If the power ever went out, you could estimate how long it'd been out by how much of the ice had melted and how far the penny had fallen. It was at the bottom. The power must've been out *all* night.

The meat still felt somewhat cool, and while the cardboard of the frozen boxes of food were soggy, the contents were still cool to the touch as well. But, he'd have to cook everything right away.

His shoulders slumped on the way back to the living room. He was going to have a long day.

And he could forget a shower. Without power, he didn't have water either. At least not good, clean water readily available, unless he wanted to raid his preps. But one way or the other though, he'd have to at least figure out how to get some coffee going. Quick, too. His head was pounding already.

He re-focused on the iPad. Still no connection to the internet. He clicked to try to re-connect and patiently watched it cycle through three more retries and countdowns.

Not working. *No internet service either?*

The letters: E M P screamed through his head again.

The keys to his truck were on the table. He snatched them up and hurried—as much as he could while limping —through the eerily silent, dark house to the driveway, with Ozzie following behind him.

Could this really be happening? He'd prepared for it for years, but when one after another crisis passed with not much more than a wrinkle, he'd almost began to believe— just like the sheeple—that no end of the world event would ever happen in his lifetime after all. This past year he'd been lackadaisical in his prepping. Had he even rotated the expired canned goods this year? Had he reminded Jake to treat the fuel tank lately?

A sweat broke out on his forehead. He slid barefoot into the driver's side of his truck with his heart pounding. If someone had asked him a year ago if he was 'prepared' for an EMP, he would have said yes. But that was a year ago. Now? He wasn't so sure.

He inserted the key and turned it, holding it there much longer than necessary.

"If this *is* it, it's gonna leave a mark," he mumbled.

THE TRUCK STARTED!

He slammed his hand against the steering wheel.

Damn, I must be losing my mind... panicking over a power outage?

He laughed at himself, realizing he was more affected by his wife not being home than he thought he had been. Jumpy. Paranoid. He wasn't even going to mention this to her when she returned.

But still...

No power in the house.

No cell phone service.

No internet services.

It really *could* have finally happened. Maybe it wasn't an EMP, but the news had been filled with reports of smaller cyber-attacks. Accusations had been thrown far and wide, including against Russia whose president denied the accusations, but was getting seriously pissed about it. The

Russian president was a proud and scary man, and the memes and funny jokes posted all around the world of his 'relations' with America's new president had to be rankling his skin.

In fact, Grayson had seen a special report just yesterday that warned Russia's good diplomacy toward the new president—which Russia had been accused of helping into office by hacking into our systems and swiping strategic bits to share with WikiLeaks in order to shape United States politics—was flipping. If Russia had indeed helped the new president win the election, the president wasn't returning the favors. Within his first six months in office, he'd not only given the Russian president the cold shoulder, but he'd also slapped them with several new sanctions, bombed one of their allies and given no quarter toward the Russian president or his country, as far as anyone could see.

If they had been in bed together, the honeymoon was definitely over between Russia and America's president.

Another channel had been reporting sporadic power outages country-wide due to system hacks, as well as breaches to national security information files. This particular news channel implied the Chinese were the culprits, warning that while China hadn't yet launched an *attack*, exactly, but that they were engaged in "passive intelligence-collection activity"—otherwise known as cyber*espionage.*

After two years of hearing both sides of the political parties whine and cry about unsecured emails, system hacking, and cyber-stuff, he'd mostly tuned it out as just noise. Like probably millions of other Americans, he'd flipped the channel after only a few moments, looking for something more entertaining.

The more he thought about it, the more he realized he'd been seeing and hearing *a lot* of threats to the electrical grid and entire infrastructure of the United States. But he hadn't really paid attention. As soon as the talking heads started talking, he'd flip to Alaskan survival shows or start another Netflix binge.

When had Americans become so desensitized that they ignored news reports like that? Maybe that was the plan? Bombard television and social media with possibilities, threats, what-ifs and maybe's so that we stopped listening and our guard went down and they could really catch us all with our pants down. What better way to cripple a country? Fight an invisible war with no boots on the ground? Let the country implode around itself without firing the first bullet or nuclear weapon? It could be done with little to no loss of life and/or money to the attacker.

So what if *it* had finally happened?

It wasn't like he hadn't warned his friends and family that *something* could happen so many times that he'd felt like Chicken Little. Or *The Little Boy Who Cried Wolf*.

Bloody hell.

Maybe this really was it. He had a gut feeling it was *something*.

Something more than just a typical power outage.

Blood coursed faster through his veins, fueled by a sudden shot of adrenaline. His heart slammed against his chest, scaring him more than a little. All the beer, chili and junk food lately—not to mention the bacon he ate four or five times a week for breakfast—made him a prime candidate for a heart attack. He clutched his chest in panic.

If he was right, and this was the fabled *teotwawki,* it was going to be bad. He was a prepper; so he was more prepared than the average Joe. But no damn good it did him when his family wasn't *here.* He'd never seriously considered that possibility.

Ozzie whined outside the truck, unsure if they were going somewhere, and not wanting to miss out on a ride. Grayson dropped his head to the steering wheel and took in several deep breaths. No use getting worked up *if* this was it. He knew what to do. They all did. Everyone had a job to do and they had a somewhat solid plan. His was to get the house ready. Theirs was to just *get home.*

Olivia and her sisters were at the beach, his daughter at university in Columbia, and Jake and Dusty hopefully were just in town; at least they were local.

He wondered if his little brother, Dusty—who was married to Olivia's little sister, Emma—would come immediately to the homestead, or if Dusty would be wrapped up in police stuff.

Grayson breathed in relief when he realized Rickey, Dusty's stepson, was with him. Emma would have his hide if he didn't bring the kid directly here if this was the real deal. *Yeah... he'll come here first; police business next—if ever.*

With no way to communicate with his family, he hoped they'd all figure it out *if* this wasn't a typical power outage. If they waited too long to leave and head home, there was no telling what they'd run into. Especially the women. And his little girl.

A chill ran down his spine.

He slowly shook his head from side to side.

If this *was* it, his long-awaited plan had failed on the first day.

3

THE LADIES – TWO DAYS LATER

"SHIT... MEET FAN," Gabby announced as she hovered over her twin sister, Olivia, casting a long shadow.

"Shit meet sand, don't you mean?" Emma said and laughed.

While Gabby tried not to stare, it was hard *not* to see several people squatting out on the dunes. Men. Women. Children. No one was exempt from bodily functions, and after days of being stuck in their rooms, many had realized house-keeping wasn't coming back. If they wanted to continue to sleep in their hotel rooms, they'd have to *use the bathroom* outside. All the public restrooms in the hotel were *beyond* 'out of service,' too.

Mothers had confiscated their children's sand shovels to dig cat-holes, while the kids stood wiggling in place uncomfortably, tear-stained faces shining. Make-shift screens were thrown up with daddies holding beach towels or umbrellas and then taken right down. Everything was valuable now. Couldn't afford to leave it up to help others who may not have a towel or umbrella. It was every man for himself and this was the hardest part—so far—for the children, especially the young ones who not that long ago were trained to *only* potty in a private toilet. Teenagers were even more hesitant. They'd rather plan their own funeral than poo in public. It was hard on everyone.

Several small groups of people were clustered around pots or large bowls covered in saran wrap. Inside the pot or bowl would be another smaller bowl, in which to catch the excruciatingly slow dripping condensation from the salt water they were trying to desalinate to drink. Right now, it was mostly all fun and games and wannabe survivalists tried to show off their skills.

Soon, it would become deadly serious.

Gabby exchanged rueful glance with Emma. Neither one of them wanted to get involved with strangers but someone should tell them it would take all day to fill a small container up like that, and it wasn't enough for even one person to survive on. They were only making things worse for themselves sitting in the hot sun and sweating. They needed more containers. Lots more, and set out in a safe and sunny place that wouldn't require people standing over to watch in the hot sun.

Like maybe on their balconies?

Duh.

And then there was their sister, Olivia, doing her own bit of avoidance. In the resort, they were sheltered from the madness and chaos running rampant in the already-crazy tourist town of Myrtle Beach. But several people had left the resort and reported back that things were nucking futs out there; looting, fighting, and worse was going on outside the resort gates. Emma and Gabby had wandered out themselves and hurriedly returned. After what they saw, there was no doubt it was time to get out of Dodge, before things got worse. They certainly weren't going to get any better.

Gabby crossed her arms, fuming that Olivia was just *sitting* there on the beach, paperback in her lap, enjoying the sights and sounds of the ocean, while she and Emma had worn themselves out walking in the hot sun. They had hoped to find at least one gas station nearby that still had gas and a generator to pump it. Or water. They'd found nothing. Gabby had wanted to venture out further, but neither of them had wanted to leave Olivia behind in her little bubble of denial for too long.

Olivia gave her identical twin sister a bored look. "What now, Gabby? Fire and brimstone raining down from the sky?" She looked from Gabby to their little sister, Emma, and took a long sip of water.

Great. Now we're down to three bottles, Gabby thought. They were the lucky ones. They'd brought along a case of water to keep in their room for the trip. But their supply was quickly dwindling down.

Emma smiled at Olivia patiently.

They all knew it was time to leave. Olivia was just being stubborn, refusing to believe this could possibly be the event that her own husband has been preparing for; that they'd *all* helped to prepare for. Apparently, she had thought it had all been for fun and games for them to learn to shoot, and to can veggies and the other dozens of survival skills that her own husband, Grayson, had insisted they try. A fun hobby. Something to do to bring them together as a family. She probably never thought this would *really* happen.

Gabby swung her long, brown hair over her shoulder and put her hands on her hips. She looked to her little sister, Emma, who stood beside her for support. Emma was their little mini, except she was eight years younger—in her mid-twenties—and four inches shorter. She shared the same slender build, long dark hair and blue eyes. If it wasn't for the height, they could pass as triplets, even with the age gap between her and the twins.

Emma shrugged, not yet ready to choose sides between the twins.

"Olivia, I'm serious," Gabby said. "I think this might really be it. Remember those loud noises we heard after the power went out? Some of the other guests said it was transformers exploding. This is more than just a power outage. If you walk out of the resort and up the road, you can still see smoke. There's buildings on fire. Things are crazy out there. They're going to get worse. We need to get home."

Olivia shook her head. "It's been two days, Gabby. Give them time to find the problem and get the power back on. Let's wait it out, get a good night of peaceful sleep tonight and see if things are back on tomorrow. *I'm* not leaving our vacation. Don't be silly. What are we going to do, walk two hundred miles home?"

She faced the ocean again, watching the waves roll in and break against her feet. She wiggled her toes, poking the carefully manicured red tips up out of the sand, as though she didn't have a care in the world... just another day at the beach, *la-la la-la la...*

Gabby wanted to slap sense into her. They *needed* to get moving. Grayson had always predicted if this ever happened, it would probably be only two or three days before all hell broke loose and people lost their minds— and their humanity. Then it would be TEOTWAWKI: the end of the world as we know it. And Emma's husband, Dusty, had agreed. He was a cop for Pete's sake. How much more validation did Olivia need?

"It's not just the power. It's the internet, too. And phone service. *All* communications. We're cut off here from the world. Ever known that to happen before? So yes, that's exactly what we're going to have to do. *Walk.* Because you didn't want to fill up with gas before checking in and now, there is no gas to be had. And that's not all, either. Not only is it the electricity, phones, *air-condition*, and internet. It's water, too. Water is the game-changer. We really have to leave now because the hotel is *out* of water—and food. All the water we have is what's left in our room. And here you sit in the hot sun, drinking it. We've got to head home," she insisted.

Olivia looked at her watch. She shrugged. "I've heard a few cars leaving. We just need to find gas wherever they're finding it." She pointed out to the ocean, where the sun was beginning to drop fast, spreading its pink, orange and red coloring across the horizon. "And we've got more water than we need right there."

Gabby huffed and took in a deep breath, blowing it out in frustration.

Emma put her hand on Gabby's arm, letting her know she'd try. "Olivia, the people you saw leaving may have had gas when they left here, but they won't get far before they need more, and there isn't any. The gas stations that *did* still have gas were charging up to a hundred dollars a gallon cash only, and even that went fast. It's gone now. We're stranded—"

Gabby interrupted. "And we can't drink saltwater. You know that. We don't have any idea how to do it. It's not just boiling water, ya know? There's *salt* to get out of the water, too. We could use the condensation trick, but that'd take forever to get just a tiny bit to drink."

She waved her arms slowly to indicate the beach. "There's just not enough resources here. There's too many people. We have to go somewhere else. Emma and I just came from the resort snack bar and restaurant. We stood for over an hour waiting to get in and just before our turn, they hung up a *closed* sign. They're out. No more *food* either. We're going to have to walk farther to find some. All we have is what's in our room—our unbearably hot, stinky room. The maids aren't coming. No more water is coming. No more *food*. No magic genie who can turn saltwater into drinking water or gas. If we've got to go find food and water for ourselves anyway, we may as well do that on the way *home*."

Gabby stopped long enough to take a breath, but Emma held up her hand to take a turn, "Olivia, she's right. We've got to leave now. Things are getting worse. You can't change it by denial. Your own husband has been telling you this could happen. Grayson would be so disappointed in you for stalling." She pursed her lips and slowly shook her head at Olivia. "And what about Graysie stuck an hour from home at college? I'll bet she's not just sitting there with her head—or feet—in the sand thinking someone is going to turn the power back on. She's probably on the way home, too."

Olivia abruptly stood up, the back of her legs knocking her chair over in the sand. "Fine! But how the heck are we —three women—going to walk all the way home? Two hundred miles. Have you two lost your minds? We aren't nineteen years old like Graysie, and this isn't just a lap around the mall or a hot yoga class." She waved her hands around. "This is...it's... insane. We're talking hot asphalt and pavement, dusty roads, and woods. Lots of woods. Do you seriously think we can make it all the way there on *foot*?" Olivia's voice wavered on the last sentence and her chin trembled.

Seems she was a little more bothered than she'd been letting on after all.

Emma nodded emphatically while Gabby smiled and hugged her twin sister, knowing she was coming around —finally.

"We can find a way," Gabby insisted. "The only other option is to stay here, and you know the guys are probably worrying themselves to death about us. I'm sure Rickey is safe with Dusty, but I'll bet he's worried about his mama." She gave Emma a sympathetic look. "Let's pull up our big girl panties and show them we *were* listening for the past two years. I've got my bug-out bag in the room, and both of yours are in the car. We've got guns. I think we can do it."

Olivia grimaced. "Yeah, I need to talk to you about those bags."

Before Gabby or Emma could respond, they were knocked over by a man running between them awkwardly swinging a heavy ice chest. As the girls tumbled to the sand in a heap and another man...and another...ran through them, giving chase.

"Hey! Watch it," Gabby yelled after them. "There's women and children—"

Bang Bang Bang

Shots fired out and the beach erupted in screams and a scurry of people grabbing children and running away toward the beach access ramp, sprinting toward safety in a panic. In seconds the once spread-out crowd who'd only dotted the sand every fifty to hundred feet were now running toe to heel, clustered together and bottlenecking at the access ramp to the resort. Some were jumping the fence over the dunes, others shoving to get through the gate onto the boardwalk. People kicked and screamed. Women and children were crying.

Total chaos in seconds.

Another *Pop Pop Pop* and the crowd roared and surged, doubling their efforts to get away.

Emma stayed down, hands over her head as the gritty sand, dirty feet, heavy coolers, and brightly-striped towels flashed past them. Gabby was on her knees, her head spinning side to side, trying to look around knees and ankles for the shooter.

Now people were running *back* to the beach—some of them. Others were still running away—causing the crowd to crash and buckle. People fell down. Tangles of limbs. Screams rang out through the air. The terrified cries of children rose above the pandemonium.

Gabby struggled to her feet and shielded her eyes with her hand, squinting to look down the beach. Was it something that came from down there? What was happening? She didn't see anyone pointing a gun...maybe it was just fireworks?

She turned to ask Emma and Olivia if they saw anything.

But Olivia wasn't thinking.

She wasn't doing anything; sprawled in the sand on her back with a trickle of blood running down the side of her head, she looked like she was finally getting some peaceful sleep.

Gabby screamed.

4

JAKE

"YEAH, I'M A DAMN APOCALOPTOMIST ALRIGHT."

Jake ran his hands over his face, and kept on the whispered rant against himself, "I *know* the shit has probably hit the fan but I'm playin' like it's all gonna be alright. Way to be a good neighbor, Jake," he said out loud to himself. He slammed his fist against the wall. He felt like crap for lying. He cringed as he thought about the conversation.

The idiot neighbor—the one that had been driving him crazy for years with his unkempt grass, stupid mulch-straw mounds with nothing growing in them, and once, even putting a beekeepers box in his back yard that had been bothering Gabby the entire summer until they'd discovered it—had knocked on his door an hour ago. When he'd answered it, Kenny had asked him what he should do with all the food in his freezer that was defrosting. Jake had just shrugged and said, "Eat it or throw it out, I guess."

He'd played stupid.

Kenny had asked him if he thought the power was coming back on and Jake had shrugged again and said, "Sure. I guess it will, eventually."

He'd lied through his teeth. His brothers-in-law, both Grayson and Dusty—who coincidentally were actual brothers—had been telling him for a long time that this could happen. And if it did, the power wasn't coming back on for quite a while. Kenny, and a lot of the people in this neighborhood, were clueless.

Most of them lived in their McMansions, drove high-priced cars and kept less than a week's worth of food on hand. Heck, some of them probably less than that. They probably didn't have the first idea of what they should be doing. That food needed to be cooked, canned or dehydrated. They needed to conserve food, and especially water.

They were just lucky the power had gone out at night, while most of them were in their beds sleeping, and that they weren't having to trudge home on foot from their high-falootin' jobs.

He sighed. Although he was well-liked by everyone here, he'd never felt at home. When Gabby had found the house and fell in love with it, he'd agreed to move here for her. She was making good money in her job, and he was doing okay as a mechanic, so they could afford the place, but they were surrounded by doctors, lawyers and company-owners—people who made a lot more money than they did, and lived a different lifestyle.

They'd made a few close friends, like Tucker and Katie.

But mostly they kept to themselves. Even so, as a mechanic, he seemed to be the guy that everyone came to for all questions regarding small engines, broken irrigation, and appliances. Probably because he didn't hesitate to lend a hand whenever someone needed it and had a knack for figuring most anything out. He wasn't surprised Kenny had come to him. There'd probably be more knocks on the door.

He glanced out the window just in time to see the neighbor across the street dump a bucket of what he assumed to be dirty water onto a blue hydrangea. *Just wasted it... unreal.* Jake rubbed his hands over his face again and looked away. He couldn't watch anymore.

Of all times for Gabby to take off on a vacation with her sisters. It'd been *two* days. Two days of no communication with her, or anyone. Two *long* days of him sitting alone, hoping the power was coming back on, yet knowing it probably wasn't. He knew he should be getting busy. There was so much to do, and he should be helping Grayson out at the homestead.

He just couldn't get his head together. Couldn't stop worrying about Gabby and the girls. Couldn't stop hoping the power was coming back on. But mostly it was about Gabby. He'd been laid out on the couch, avoiding the neighbors most of the past two days, frozen with anxiety over his wife.

Admit it, Jake, there's more than that keeping you glued to the couch.

Jake shook that thought away. He wouldn't admit it. To

admit it would give it power over his life. No, he refused to think of that right now.

He pushed his secret back down, before it got away from him.

He rubbed his knuckles and was surprised to see blood over his oil-stained creases. *Crap.* Not cool in a grid-down situation to purposely hurt yourself. He stomped into the bathroom and grabbed the big brown bottle of peroxide. He poured it over his hand, let it bubble a moment, and then shook it off. It was time to get the heck out of there. If Grayson had been right these past few years, the shit was about to hit the fan. The news had been predicting it, if you listened hard enough.

He'd heard the talk from the neighborhood, too, on the first day. One woman worked across the border, for American Airlines in Charlotte, North Carolina. She said all planes were grounded. Not only were the flight plans usually electronic, but all their ground systems were too. No power or communications meant no air transportation. It was utter chaos at Charlotte Douglas Airport, according to her. She'd wasted her gas getting to work only to be turned around and sent home, barely squeaking into her driveway on empty, too afraid to attempt getting any more gas while she was alone.

She'd said the lines at the gas stations she'd passed were filled with angry people. There were only a few that had generators running to pump the gas, and fights had broken out over the limited supply. Only cash was accepted and they were fleecing people for a five-gallon limit.

Another neighbor worked for the power company. Rumor was the system *was* hacked. A cyber-attack. Not only did they not have control of it yet to bring it back up, but dozens of transformers around town had blown. With the number needed, it would take a *long* time to get those in, as most big parts were made in China, and that was if they could repair the hack and take back control of the system.

The fire departments were using every drop of gas they had stored up to locate and fight fires, from blown transformers. Soon, they wouldn't be able to go anywhere either. It was rumored that by late evening yesterday, there was no gas in town, according to the neighborhood chatter.

Great day.

No phones. No cars. No power. No running water.

No shit?

He shook his head. It was time to stop procrastinating and hoping it wasn't real.

It. Was. Real.

He had a plan. He wasn't a tree, he could move if he wanted to. If he tried hard enough. He just had to get motivated to *get* moving. Grayson was probably chomping at the bit by now wondering where he was. He'd have to come up with a good excuse for sitting around doing nothing up until now. He couldn't tell him the *real* reason. No one could know that. No one *would* know that; especially his wife, Gabby.

He passed their bed and glanced at the bed-side table. There was his motivation. He stepped over and picked up their wedding picture. She had been eighteen years old. A child-bride. Her long-brown hair and sapphire eyes had mesmerized him from the moment he'd met her. Now she —and her twin—were in their early thirties, and they were more beautiful than they'd been at eighteen. Same long hair, same blue eyes. And their little sister, Emma, looked just like them.

Jake shook his head and swallowed hard. *What the hell is wrong with me? Women like this out on the road during this chaos?* His pulse quickened as a thousand bad scenarios flashed through his brain. He took a deep breath, trying to calm himself. It wouldn't do to get all worked up. They were probably doing the same thing everyone else was, sitting around waiting for the lights to come back on. It would be sometime in the next few days that they would realize they'd have to hoof it.

His eyes slid to the ball cap also resting on the table. It was Gabby's favorite. The emblem on the front and the three letters: TSS, stood for *The Shooting Sisterhood*. It was an online group of women who loved guns and shooting. Gabby had joined it over a year ago. She kept in regular contact through Facebook with her 'sisters in shooting,' who all encouraged and supported each other. Gabby had mentioned a few were gathering here, at their local gun range to shoot together this week in a tournament and she'd been disappointed about having to miss it—but shooting couldn't compete with the beach with her real blood sisters. He felt guilty that he'd encouraged her to go.

He'd wanted time alone to try to deal with his own demons. To try to crush them before he was crushed.

He hadn't made any headway after all.

Now, he wished she'd stayed home for the tournament.

He grabbed the hat and loosened it to fit his own head. He pulled it down tight and breathed in the scent of his wife's hair. A good reminder for him to stay motivated and moving. He needed to haul his ass over to Grayson's. He knew without a doubt Grayson would say the plan has always been in an event or a crisis, for everyone to head to the homestead.

But he didn't know if he could wait for Gabby any longer. Maybe he and Grayson should try to get to the girls —before someone else did.

5

GRAYSIE

Graysie swung her long, curly red hair over her shoulder —the way only a nineteen-year-old co-ed could—and straightened the sign on the bathroom door between the dorm-suites. It read: 'If it's yellow, let it mellow. If it's brown, flush it down.'

She rolled her eyes. Her dad, Grayson, had used the same phrase when the power had gone out at home for one long icy weekend. She scrunched her nose up to enter. The lid was down. She hopped in place as she looked for something to lift it with. With this smell, she didn't want to touch it.

Perfect, we're out of toilet paper.

She'd known two rolls wouldn't last long with three suite-mates in her dorm, and sure enough the cardboard roll sat naked and dejected on the holder.

So nice of them to save me some.

She used the edge of her flip-flop to lift the toilet lid and nearly gagged. So much for the sign. No wonder it smelled so bad in here. Someone hadn't flushed down their 'brown.' She grimaced as she looked around for their bucket of water. The college administrators had offered water to anyone that could provide something to put it in. Thank goodness one of her roommates had a clean fetish and kept a bucket in their room to wash her car. Without the water, they couldn't flush at all. As she looked at the mess, she wondered why that fetish didn't apply here.

She spied the bucket in the corner, filled with damp towels. *Are you freaking kidding me?* Someone had used the last of the water to bathe? She gathered her hair in her hand and brought it over her shoulder. She shook her head in disgust as she turned around and sat down. She couldn't hold it any longer.

She breathed out a sigh of relief as she let her bladder go and cringed as she took in a new breath; the smell was awful. Only forty-eight hours and already it was unbearable. Between the stale, hot temperature of their room, the lack of a clean, working toilet, and the slapdash demeanor of the other students, she was ready to do something. *Anything.* She had to get out of there. If she could just make it past the security guard, she'd find a way home. It was only a little over an hour drive to her dad's farm. How long would that take to walk? Maybe she could ride a bike?

But again—the security guard. She couldn't believe the administration was trying to keep them here. They'd said, 'for your own good.' Good God, she was nineteen years old. That was old enough to join the freaking army, yet not old enough to be released during an emergency without parent's permission? Who made that stupid rule? Graysie didn't believe they could really hold them there. One old fart with a gun against a whole dorm? *Yeah, right.* It probably wasn't even a real gun anyway.

She could probably put on her heels, make up her face, and saunter right in and make him believe she was just crossing to another dorm. Then she could high-tail it out of there. But she couldn't leave empty-handed. And she couldn't leave in heels. There was no way to get Sally—her Mustang—out of the secured lot, so she might be walking all the way home.

She sighed as she pulled her shorts up and looked for the hand-sanitizer. She couldn't wash her hands, but at least it was something. She placed her hand under it and pumped.

Empty.

Dammit. They'd used all of that too. *Thanks, ladies.*

She stomped into their room with her hands on her hips. Becky had come back while she was in the bathroom and now she was on the bottom bunk—Graysie's bed— brushing out her fake-blonde hair and reading a book. Her hair was damp. Graysie wanted to rip a hunk of the long strands right out of her head.

"Get off my bed, Becky. And thanks a lot for using all the water. Now we can't flush the toilet. That's disgusting."

Becky rolled her eyes. "My *hair* was disgusting. I haven't washed it in two days. What did you expect me to do?" She slowly climbed off of Graysie's bunk, leaving strands of hair behind her with no regard. She was so clueless.

Graysie swept her hand across the bedspread, wiping the hair onto the floor. She laid down. "I expect you to go find more water to replace it. We're going to need some to drink too. We're almost out. You drank all yours too fast. I've got three bottles, and I swear if you take them, I'm going to kill you."

Becky shrugged her shoulders. "I did go. The security guard said there's no more water for the toilets, or bottled water. But I've still got a case of Monster Drink, so I don't need your yucky water. They'll have the power back on soon, anyway. And if they don't, my parents will come and get me. I've got plenty of food, too."

Graysie shook her head. Becky's food consisted of junk: Oatmeal cream pies, Ramen Noodles that required *water*, and potato chips. Nothing healthy. Nothing fresh. "No, they won't. Not unless they've stocked up on a lot of gas, and somehow, I can't see your folks stocking up on anything."

That was an understatement. Becky's family lived a charmed life in a white-bread world where everything was always available to them at the touch of a button or wave of their hand. They were filthy rich; her father was a surgeon in high demand.

"And what if the power doesn't come back on, Becky? My dad warned me about this. If the power went out everywhere all at once, there could be blown transformers. It might take more than just flipping a switch to get it back on. And most of our infrastructure is made up of parts from China. And what if it was China that hacked us? They're not gonna give us those parts. It could be *long* while before power is back on. Which means it could be awhile before roads are cleared—and I did talk to Susan's dad when he came to get her and he said it's a nightmare out there. It took him two *hours* to drive ten *miles*. Once the refineries get power, the trucks have to be fueled up, and then loaded with the fuel to be pumped into the gas stations for the public. If your parents didn't get here yet, it's because they can't. They're out of gas. May as well face it."

"We don't know if the power is out everywhere. No one does."

She had a point. Without communications, they had no idea if it was only the state capital affected, or the whole state. Or the whole country.

Becky fanned her hair out behind her and closed her eyes. "I don't know how, but they'll find a way," she mumbled in a bored voice.

Another nap. Go figure.

Graysie hadn't expected a logical answer from her anyway. Becky was a spoiled, rotten airhead. She was the princess of her world. She ate Graysie's food, used her things, left a mess everywhere, never cleaned up after herself and relied on her parents for *everything*. She didn't even have to work a part-time job. Her parents gave her $150/week allowance. She had it made.

So sure, in Becky's little mind, they'd magically appear

to take her home to their nice, air-conditioned McCastle overflowing with fresh food and drink. They'd run her right home and keep her in a fancy bubble until this all blew over and their little princess was safe and secure once more. Well, would if they could. *Good luck with that, Becky.*

She rolled her eyes and buried her face into her pillow. She had to get away before she strangled her roommate. She thought about her dad and Olivia at the farm. They had plenty of everything, and her dad was probably going nuts thinking this was the big event and wondering if she had figured that out yet. She felt bad about the years of eye-rolling and long sighs she'd given him every time he'd lectured her on what to do if something like this ever happened.

But is this really it?

If it was, it was much more serious than she was prepared for.

She gasped and sat up. Her bug-out bag! She'd been thoroughly annoyed when her dad had put it in the trunk of her car, and made her double-dog-pinky-swear she would never, *ever* take it out. Several times she'd wanted to throw it out to make room for something else, but then she'd think about the trusting look her dad had given her when they'd crossed pinkies. She couldn't break his heart —again. *Thank God!*

She grabbed her keys and rushed out, ignoring Becky's question of where was she going. She had no idea what was in that backpack, but her dad had promised that it was full of things that would help her get home if she was ever stuck somewhere. And boy, was she stuck.

Graysie practiced her sad, pitiful look on her way down the stairs to the front door where the security guard sat. She had an idea to get past him. The dude was middle aged —like her dad. If he was anything like Dad, then she had a story for him.

6

GRAYSON SWUNG the axe too hard again, getting it stuck. Just a few days without power or communications and his nerves were shot. He could barely focus on anything without worries intruding of his wife, Olivia, stranded out of town with her sisters; not to mention his daughter a hundred miles away at college. He wanted to drop everything and go after them. Bring them all home. But he couldn't. He was stuck, too.

Yesterday—when the power still hadn't come back on—he'd driven into town. His fears were confirmed. He found two stations that still had gas and a generator to pump it, but to get it you'd need to wait in line two to four hours and pay a hundred bucks a gallon. Not many people carried that kind of cash around and they couldn't get it from the ATM; those weren't working and the banks were closed. Not a good time to close the banks when nearly everyone was demanding cash only.

In the short time he'd trolled the different stations, he'd witnessed a dozen fights amongst the angry, scared people. At the first sign of guns being flashed, he'd hauled ass. He had fuel prepped at home, with enough in the tank to get back there, so he wasn't going to waste his time sitting in line, hoping they didn't run out by the time his turn rolled around. He'd gone on to the grocery store.

It was packed.

With people—not food.

The shelves were nearly empty. The cold items were totally gone. The registers all had lines a mile long and people were arguing with the cashiers over their SNAP welfare cards and debit and credit cards not working. While he wandered around looking for anything to add to his preps, panic built in the waiting crowd. The cashiers were frustrated with adding up totals on paper with calculators, and their progress was constantly thwarted by not knowing the price of most items or by the non-cash paying customers. The two cashiers that had stuck it out were near tears. Another small crowd had formed around the store manager, who finally relented. He announced he'd allow thirty dollars' worth of merchandise for anyone who had at least two forms of picture identification as well as their cards, and that it would be a slow process, as he had to write down all the information so that he could run the cards later, when the power came back on.

Grayson doubted that would ever happen.

He heard people talking, too. Rumors were flying; blue-collar workers from the power company were sent home.

Nothing they could do to get power going again from outside the main office; this was internal. Verizon and other cell phone service offices locked their doors and hung signs out: *Cell Service out until Further Notice.* Prices were already being gouged at the gas stations, both for the limited gas, and the meager remains of food and drink supplies inside. All government offices were closed.

He passed a group of men furiously kicking an ATM machine. At another bank, he saw an out of control man had run his car into the front door and was forcing his way over the hood and broken glass to get in.

Wouldn't do him any good. Any money there would be in a tightly locked vault.

He'd driven through town, only making the one stop at the grocery store, and saw nary a cop. Not one. This piqued his interest so he drove by his brother's house. Dusty was a city cop. He wasn't home. Wherever he was, Rickey surely was too. He was too young to be on his own, and the schools were closed. Dusty's truck wasn't there, so he hoped they were on their way to the homestead.

He'd hurried back to meet them, only to arrive at an empty house.

The rest of the day was spent waiting on Dusty, Rickey and Jake to arrive, and wondering if he should forfeit 'the plan' and go after the women at the beach. The risk was that *they* were already on their way back home and they wouldn't cross paths. No telling which way they'd drive home—if they drove. His wife, Olivia, had driven up there, and she was notorious for running her tank to empty before filling up. He hoped and prayed that wasn't the case this time.

After hours of beating away the loneliness and panic, he'd made his mind up. He was going to get the girls. He had gas. The tank behind the barn held plenty of gas, and the rule was if you used it, replace it. But it rarely got used, so since Jake was the mechanic in the family, Grayson had assigned him the task of keeping it treated with stabilizer when needed to keep it from going bad.

He should have done the job himself.

After he'd pulled his truck around back to fill up the tank, he'd taken a big whiff only to find it smelled rancid. He'd poured some out to double-check and sure enough, the color was off. Jake hadn't treated the gas preps.

He'd swarped and cussed up a storm.

He was housebound. He didn't even have enough gas to get back and forth to town again. With no way to communicate with them, he had to hope for the best for Olivia, Gabby and Emma. *And especially Graysie.* They were on their way. They had to be.

At least that's what he kept telling himself to keep his own panic at bay.

Not to waste a day, he decided to stick to his own plan. Getting the house ready. First necessity was water. If the power came back on, well then, it was good practice.

He hunted through his shipping container several times but couldn't find his hand-pump. They'd be needing that to use the well. He remembered paying somewhere in the area of $700 bucks for the damn thing. He knew he had it, but it wasn't there, in his shipping container he kept behind the barn, where he'd put it.

He was reaching the point of exhaustion. It'd now been two days since the power and communications went out and he'd been keeping himself in high gear waiting for his family to return while preparing to bunker down with no power for a while. He planned to build a wooden tower to elevate a 275 gallon, caged IBC water tote onto. He would run the gutters from all around the house for rain water to run into it, and let simple gravity drop it into the bathroom for a working toilet, and easy access to water for bathing or cooking. That of course would require rain, but the upcoming months were notorious for showers and thunderstorms in their area—if the outage lasted that long. But for that project, he needed some help.

At least he still had fuel in his tractor.

He also had another trick up his sleeve to easily get water out of the well with no power. It wasn't as good as the pump, but it'd get them unlimited fresh water with a very limited amount of labor. For that, he'd need to find the Amish well bucket he'd bought. It too was somewhere out in that mess of a container. It was a long skinny galvanized bucket that looked nothing like a bucket; more like a pipe. For less than a hundred bucks, it would be a life saver. A little over four-foot-long and four inches in diameter, he could pop the pressure switch off the top of his well-head, pull the pipe out and drop the long bucket in. It had a valve that opened at the bottom to let the water in, and then closed when it was full. Then he only had to pull it up. That bucket and one long rope would let them keep using their well, even if they were only able to get two gallons of water per scoop. He might even build a tripod over the well head to hook the bucket to, and add a pulley and crank handle. It would make it much easier to pull up the amount of rope that it would need to drop to the actual water in the ground, and make it convenient to let the bucket hang when not in use.

But that was going on the back burner for now. He didn't want to start that project and take apart his well until he was sure the power wasn't coming back on—or when he ran out of available prep water, whichever came first.

The 2-liter soda bottles he kept filled with water, lining the bottom of his deep freezer had worked well enough to keep things somewhat solid until he'd rolled out the old refrigerator/freezer from the storage container and got it hooked up to the propane tank. Propane-run fridges weren't common and he'd been lucky to come across one on Craigslist that he'd put back for just this sort of occasion. It wasn't pretty; Olivia would have a fit when she came home and saw it in all its retro-green glory sitting cock-eyed in her kitchen. It wasn't nearly as large as the electric fridge in the house, but it worked. He'd transferred nearly everything over, buying more time to work on other things instead of having to cook all his food at once.

At least his oversized tank of propane was still good, unlike the gasoline.

He'd nearly killed himself lugging the old refrigerator

in by himself, too. He'd wait for Jake or Dusty to get here before moving out the other one.

Getting water running and chopping and splitting firewood were priority on the list, and since he'd not been successful so far at the water, he'd spent most of his time with the wood.

He took a break from swinging the axe to wipe his face with his T-shirt. Hotter than Hades out here. He shook his head in frustration, not able to stop thinking about his water pump.

It was a damn shame that someone had taken it. And he had no idea who either. Few people knew that shipping container was even back there. Hidden from the front side by a two-story, old red barn, and from the back side by woods, it wasn't easy to see, especially since Dusty and Grayson had used leaves and limbs as templates and painted the entire thing camouflage.

The shipping container was his full-size faraday cage and he'd made sure it was grounded for an EMP—not that this *was* an EMP, but who knew what was next. The container housed things he'd been collecting for years; things that might be useful in a grid-down situation. It also held a Mule 4x4, which was nearly buried in the back. He'd have to dig it out later if he could find a way to use it. It also needed gas to run.

Dammit.

Of course, Dusty and Jake knew that pump was out there. But hell, they wouldn't take it. It was partly for them and theirs. He'd originally bought the farm for himself and his daughter, Graysie, but he'd soon married Olivia, and they all made one big family. What was his was now all of theirs. They knew that. They'd helped him work the garden, reaping the benefits right along with him when they harvested fresh fruits and vegetables.

His eyes wandered to the gardens. His veggie garden was framed on each side with raised beds that Olivia had planted. She called them her herb hills—and she wrongly pronounced herb with the 'h' like a man's name.

He felt his heart tug. She'd never been into prepping— or preparing. But she'd done a little bit of research and took the initiative to help out where she could; to be a small part of it and support him. She'd planted her very own little patch of stuff, and in typical-Olivia-needing-to-take-care-of-everyone fashion, she'd thought ahead to what she and her sisters would most want if ever the grid went down.

One bed was her hygiene garden. It covered soap, tooth-paste and deodorant. She planted soapwort, licorice and sage in it. She said the soapwort could be used for body soap, shampoo and laundry. While she hadn't put it into practice yet, she claimed the leaves and roots could be dried and put up, and would still lather later.

The Licorice Root was a transplant. She'd bought a year-old starter because it took a few years to mature enough for use. It was ready now. She'd made him test it. He'd thought it pretty cool that not only did it taste okay— kind of sweet—but after each use, you'd cut the used 'brush' away and have a clean and fresh 'toothbrush' for the next use. She'd said not only could they use the licorice

Root for a toothbrush, but it also had anti-inflammatory and antibacterial uses.

The sage was a backup to the licorice plant since she hadn't known how well it would grow. It could be used by rubbing it over gums and teeth. He didn't like it nearly as much as the licorice but it did grow quickly and more easily. He'd laughed when he'd overheard her telling the ladies she had really planted it in case they ever ran out of deodorant. It could be made into an infusion to spritz their girly parts for body odor.

As if anyone would care about that in an apocalypse.

The first year taking care of the gardens they'd been bitten nearly to death by mosquitos, and driven to near insanity with the flies. So the last bed she put in was Lemon Balm, Basil and Rosemary for mosquito and fly control. She also used the Basil and Rosemary in the kitchen for cooking. She added Garlic for its therapeutic and anti-bacterial reasons, and for adding flavor to their food.

He'd built a small picket fence around her beds so that Ozzie wouldn't get into them. She'd said some of the plants could be toxic to animals. For the whole area, Grayson had stuffed a scarecrow and hung pie-pans from its arms to try to keep out other varmints.

These gardens held memories of working the dirt, laughter, slapping at bugs, long conversations—*family time*. That's what it was all about.

But yeah, the guys all helped with the big garden, and the ladies worked the smaller beds. They'd made it fun. A hobby. And if the shit never hit the fan, it wasn't a waste. Not much went uneaten, not with a group this big.

No, not a group.

A family.

He swallowed hard. It had taken him years to build a new one after his had been ripped apart. He never thought he'd have another. He'd thought he'd finish raising Graysie alone, and spend his golden years poking around the farm all by himself.

When his little brother, Dusty, had married Emma, Grayson had come to attend the wedding on Bald Head Island as a lonely, bitter, widower. He'd lost his first wife—Graysie's mom—in Hurricane Katrina. Then he'd met Emma's older sister, Olivia, and his world had been rocked—by both her and another hurricane that had unexpectedly hit the island the night before the wedding. He'd been given the honor and the salvation of rescuing her and Ozzie from the storm.

Where he'd failed his first wife, he'd succeeded with Olivia. She'd given him hope and love where before lived regret and hurt—an aching pain he hadn't believed would ever dull. He'd loved his first wife dearly, and he'd felt like he failed her. But Olivia had redeemed him. Soon after he'd asked her to marry him, and she'd said yes.

Olivia's twin sister, Gabby, was married to Jake, a good 'ole southern boy without a dishonest bone in his body. He was a mid-thirties mechanic with a strong back and a good soul, muscular physique and a knack for fixing just about anything, mechanical or not. He had a good head on his shoulders and a kind heart. Loyal as they came. He wouldn't steal. *Ever.*

And his little brother, Dusty, had only to ask. He knew that anything Grayson had was his for the taking—as long as he replaced it or brought it back. They'd borrowed off each other all their lives. Started out trading marbles and baseball cards, and then later guns and tools. Dusty would've mentioned if he'd had a need for a pump. No way. It just had to be here. But Grayson had wasted enough time looking. He had things to do. He needed to prepare the old homestead for his family. They'd all be coming, sooner rather than later, he hoped.

Especially Graysie. He knew in his heart he'd raised that girl up right. Red-headed and stubborn as a mule, he had no doubt she'd started walking toward home already. He'd trained her to handle a gun and a crossbow, and hoped she'd been listening to all the survival shows he'd watched while she pecked away on her phone texting night after night before she went away to college. Hopefully, *some* of it had sunk in. It was disappointing she'd refused survival training, but she was a smart girl... her father's daughter. He had confidence in her, although he threw up a little in his mouth each time he thought of her out on the road, alone.

No!

He caught himself and swallowed down the bile before his fears ran away from him and pushed him into another panic attack. Graysie would never be so stupid as to try it alone. She had them college boys nipping at her heels day and night. With a figure like hers and that long, curly red hair, he hoped she'd just this once use it to her advantage to recruit a few strong boys to escort her home. Hell, he'd even let a boy stay, if he brought his daughter home unhurt and unmolested.

He'd been an idiot not telling Graysie what he'd hidden under her bed, in her dorm room. What if she didn't find it? *Dammit again.*

He shook off thoughts of Graysie, reminding himself there wasn't a thing he could do except wait. No time to worry right now.

But what about Jake and Dusty? They were an hour away, in town. He knew Dusty had his stepson, Rickey, with him, so why hadn't they gotten here yet? It was only a day's walk and the power had been out two days now. Surely, he wasn't still working with the gas shortage, and a thirteen-year old boy in tow. He imagined Dusty was pretty worked up about Emma being stuck on vacation when this happened. Maybe he'd somehow gone to get her, and taken their son with him?

He shook his head. *No way.* If he had a vehicle, he'd drop Rickey off here first. He wouldn't risk the boy to rescue the mama; Emma would kick his ass.

And Jake. Where the hell was Jake? Maybe Jake could figure out a way to salvage the gas. He was a fixer by nature and a mechanic by trade. Surely, he knew something to do? At the very least, he expected Jake to have a full tank of gas in his own truck. He should be here by now. But Jake had been acting weird lately. Not himself. Sort of down and out sometimes. He'd noticed it but assumed Gabby, Jake's wife, was on top of it.

Although Jake put on a stoic face, everyone knew he still dealt with a lot of pain from a car accident years ago. Grayson figured his up and down moods lately were related to that.

Jake and Dusty had to know he was nearly out of his mind with worry for everyone, especially the women. He jerked the ax out of the log and threw it as hard as he could. It flipped ass over elbows three times before lodging in a tree. He threw his head back and screamed, "*Where the hell are you guys*?!"

He stomped off to cool down. Pacing back and forth in the shade behind the barn where the chickens had just rounded the bend, he let off steam. He let out all his inner ramblings and fears. He directed all his anger at the absent Dusty and Jake. "What about the damn plan, guys? You two are supposed to be *here*. I can't do this all alone. I don't want to be here *by myself*. This was for all of you. Son of a bitch, Jake! We *could* be driving to get the women. What if something happens to them? What if we can't find them because you farted around getting here?"

He turned and threw his hands up in the air. "And where the hell are *you*, Dusty? I *need* you, brother. I. Need. You," he screamed at the top of his lungs.

The chickens that had been ignoring him scattered in the wind.

He leaned against the barn, out of breath. He slid down the wall onto his rear end, sitting on the ground with his head in his hands. His bad tooth was giving him hell, too. He rubbed his jaw. He'd obviously missed his dentist appointment.

Ozzie, the dog, slowly slunk over, his head down and tail between his legs. He sniffed in Grayson's direction, took a few more steps, and dropped next to him. He lay his head in Grayson's lap, coaxing a pat from the anguished man.

One reluctant pat turned into more petting. Grayson couldn't resist the big brown eyes looking up at him. "Damn dog. Been moping around for days looking for your mama, haven't ya?" he said, his voice breaking. "Me, too, buddy."

Eyes turned up toward the sky, trying to clear them of their sudden blurriness, he breathed out long and hard. And then in again—a short, sucking breath. He dropped his head, wrapped his arms around Ozzie and pulled him close. He hugged the dog. Ozzie whimpered so he loosened his grip. The dog settled beside him and wagged his tail.

Grayson knew his face was blood-red, he could feel the heat of it. His heart beat wildly, thumping against his chest. His blood pressure was up too high. He'd held it together for close to two days, but being out here alone, with only the dog for company—driving him crazy whining for Olivia —he was falling apart.

This wasn't the way it supposed to happen. Shit was going to get real in a few days—maybe even today. It could get ugly. They needed to get the house ready. They needed to be *together*. He needed his wife and daughter. He needed them here, with him. Without them, he had no reason for any of this. Yet they were stuck out there somewhere, with the crazies and the yahoos, and probably worse. And there wasn't a damn thing he could do about it.

Damn it all. He felt something wet on his cheek. *What the hell?* He looked up again to see if something was dripping off the barn. *Nope.* His vision blurred once more. He blinked, spilling another tear. He laughed.

Tears? I'm crying? What the hell? I haven't cried since my momma died.

He laughed at himself again. Now, for just a moment, he was glad he was alone. It wouldn't do for anyone to see him cry. Yeah, he'd lost his shit. And he knew this was probably the last time it could ever happen. They'd come, and they'd expect him to be in control. Like he always was. The oldest, the wisest, and the meanest. But they also knew he'd protect them and get shit done. That was the way he was. That was what was expected from a git-er-done kinda guy.

A calmness settled over him. Not sure if it was because of Ozzie, or just releasing some much-needed angst, he gave the credit to the dog. "Good boy, Ozzie. Good boy." He rubbed behind Ozzie's ears as he leaned his own head back against the old red paint. He deserved a break. He'd get back on it in ten.

OLIVIA SLOWLY BLINKED her eyes until her twin sister's face came into focus.

"What," she muttered groggily. "What's wrong?" she asked Gabby, who was kneeled over next to her, crying.

"Olivia!" Gabby screamed, and pulled her close.

Olivia pushed her away. "Stop! What? What are you crying about?" she asked, looking around at the chaos with a confused look. "Where's everyone going?"

Emma separated them, pulling on Olivia's arm to get her up. "Come on. We've got to get out of here. You were hit in the head, probably by a cooler. It knocked you out. Shots have been fired. We need to go. Get up."

Olivia eyes widened. "Shots?"

Emma looked around in a panic. "Gun shots. So, hurry. I think whoever was shooting is gone now, but we need to get off the beach to somewhere safe. Let's go back to the room."

Olivia felt her head—her hand came away sticky and wet. She gasped and looked to her twin sister, Gabby. "This is why you're crying? You thought I was shot or something?"

Gabby cleared her throat and jumped to her feet. She turned as though looking behind her and discreetly swiped her tears away, and then reached down a hand for Olivia. "No, stupid. I was crying because you're wearing *my* favorite bikini. It's ruined now. Forget it. Let's go."

Olivia looked down at the black and white suit, now black and white with red splatters of her own blood dotting it. Emma shook her head at Gabby, seeing right past her charade. Gabby was trying to save face.

Olivia accepted the hands of her sisters, wobbling a bit when she was on her feet, and offered Gabby a short apology. "Sorry. I'll replace it," she mumbled.

"Damn right you will. Come on. We need to take care of that cut on your head."

The girls hurried off the beach toward their room.

The man who'd been in the room next to them passed by in the hall. He was dragging a rolling suitcase and had a carry-on case slung over his shoulder. This guy had an old classic car, and they'd passed him several times on the way to the beach, arriving within minutes of each other. He obviously was coming from the same area that they had. She couldn't remember where they'd started seeing him on the road, but they'd definitely passed each other several times in the last few hours of travel. Gabby and the girls had been surprised when they saw his car parked next to them in the parking deck. It was an even bigger coincidence when he was assigned a room on the same hallway as theirs. But they hadn't spoken to him at all before now, not wanting to get his hopes up—they were all married after all—and he didn't look like the type of guy to just have a friendly conversation with.

Later, the girls had seen lots of classic cars cruising the main strip, and heard that there was a show going on. Probably a hundred or more were at the beach right now.

The man's hands were full and he had his keys in his mouth as he rolled past them. He looked fifty—trying to be forty—exhausted, sweaty, red-faced and breathing hard. He gave them a brisk nod and kept walking.

"Wait!" yelled Gabby.

The man turned around.

"Where are you going? Do you have gas?"

"*Shhh!*" The man looked around to see who had heard her and then dropped his suitcase to give the ladies his full attention. After looking them over from head to toe, he smiled, patting his thinning-hair in place and tugging the wrinkles out of his Tommy Bahama tropical orange with green palm trees shirt. A tacky gold chain lay nestled on a bed of too-much-too-gray-chest-hair. He gave them a million-dollar smile—or at least a few grand, seeing as how his fake teeth looked like a pack of perfect bleached-chiclets against his leathery-dark tan. "Yeah, I do now. I'm not leaving my girl here. I'm driving her home. She's a classic 1970 Plymouth *Roadrunner*. Top of the line. She won some awards at the show here. Want to walk out and look at her before I take off?" He beamed, waiting for their *oohs* and *awws*.

Gabby rolled her eyes. Looks like they had a real ladies man on their hands. "I don't really care what kind of car it is. We need a ride home. Where you headed?"

Ladies-Man grabbed his things and started walking backward. "Nope. I can't be giving everyone a ride. I've spent the last eight hours buying gas one can at a time. Didn't find enough so I had to crawl under a few cars and siphon it out with a screwdriver and an oil pan. Had to funnel it into cans, and had to walk and carry it back myself. Spent the last of my cash and nearly broke my back, too. But I've got plenty now to get me home and I'm not making any detours. I'm outta here."

"Wait!" Olivia said. She hurried to him, throwing a mean look at Gabby from over her shoulder. "I'm sorry, my sister is snappy. She's dehydrated and hungry. The thing is, I've been hurt." She rubbed her head to show him, not aware that her injury was painfully obvious already. "We really need to get home. You said you used the last of your cash? We've got cash. We can pay."

"I don't want cash. I was glad to get rid of most of my own." He laughed. "Those suckers don't know in a few days, cash will be worthless. That gas was worth a hundred times what I paid for it, and I paid out the ass."

"What will you take in exchange for a ride then? How can we pay?"

Ladies-Man gave her another reptilian smile, his eyes wandering down. "Well, if you need a ride that bad—"

"—we don't. Forget it!" Gabby snapped and pushed her way in front of Olivia.

He shrugged and turned to walk away again, the leer sliding from his face.

"No, wait," Olivia said. "My watch. It's a Rolex. It's got to be worth a fortune in gold and silver alone. And it has diamonds on the face. You can use it to trade."

Ladies-Man held out his hand. Olivia hurried to take it off. She held it up to him. He reached for it but Gabby reached in and snatched it away. "You can have it when you get us home."

Ladies-Man thought a moment while he looked over the girls one by one, moving his eyes quickly away from Gabby's venomous stare and back to Olivia and Emma, who were both staring at him in desperate hope. "Alright. I'm going as far as McBee, South Carolina. Don't know where you're going, but I'll drop you off there. That's about a hundred miles. That's the only deal I'm making—and it's in exchange for the watch."

Gabby walked the other way. "No, thanks. That's only halfway home. Not worth it. We'll find someone else who'll give us a ride, and won't make us pay for it with a fifteen-thousand-dollar watch—or anything else," she snapped.

"*Fifteen-thousand-dollar* watch?" Ladies-Man asked. "Look, we got off on the wrong foot. I'm Larry." He gestured stupidly to himself. Like who the hell else would be Larry? "I'll take you ladies all the way home in exchange for the watch but I'll need enough gas to get back home myself. Do you think you can do that? It might mean siphoning any gas you have in any of your husbands or family or friends' cars, deal?" he asked as he looked at their ring fingers, all which were adorned with wedding rings.

"Yes," Emma and Olivia both happily said in unison.

Gabby rolled her eyes.

Olivia was overjoyed. "Of course! My husband keeps a lot of gas stored. He's a prep—"

"—a *puppy* groomer, she meant to say. She fumbles her words sometimes," Gabby interrupted. "Olivia's husband does mobile dog grooming so he probably has a tank full of gas and I doubt he's working. He's probably too worried about us."

Olivia gave Gabby a what-the-tarnation-are-you-talk-ing-about-look, until suddenly her eyebrows raised and her eyes widened. "Yes, puppy groomer is what I meant to say. I'm sure the van is topped off. My husband always fills it up before coming home. When are we leaving?"

"Twenty minutes. And no suitcases. My trunk is full of gas. You can hold a bag in your lap. I'll meet you in the parking deck. Look for a—"

"—we know what your car looks like. We passed you on the way here," Gabby interrupted.

"Oh. Well then. Twenty minutes." He hurried away.

"We've got to take our suitcases. Gabby, you think you can make him change his mind?" Olivia asked.

"No. And we don't want to be stuck out on the road with no gas. We'll just grab your bug-out bags from your car after we grab a few things from the room." She pushed the door open to their room. "Anyone got some sort of bag we can put some things in here?"

Olivia groaned. "My beach bag! I left it out on the beach. And it's got my phone in it."

Gabby shook her head. "Too late. No time."

The ladies ran around grabbing essentials. Emma and Gabby grabbed their cell phones—even though they were useless for anything other than looking at their photo galleries.

Olivia grabbed the extra water and the few snacks they had left. They all snatched up their make-up bags, and grabbed clothes from their open suitcases, throwing everything into a pile on the bed as they worked. Gabby spun around, looking for anything else they needed. Emma had her sneakers in her hand, Olivia had her flip-flops— "Wait. Don't take your flip-flops, Olivia. What if we have to walk?" Gabby asked.

"I don't have anything any more comfortable. These are Rainbows; they'll be fine."

Gabby sighed. "Just hurry. We don't want him to leave without us. Where's a bag?"

Emma threw up her hands and shrugged. Olivia shook her head.

"Geez. Give me your biggest T-shirts. I'll make us a bag just to carry this to the parking deck, and we can grab your BOB's and transfer some things into those, if they'll fit. I hope they're bigger than mine. But we're not taking anything out of them; especially not the guns and ammo. If there was ever a time we needed those survival bags, it's now. Thank God Grayson made us each get one."

Olivia shuffled back a step. "Did I mention I needed to talk to you guys about those bags? I...er...didn't bring them," she stammered.

8

JAKE

JAKE TIED the last bungee cord around his small bag, fastening it just in front of the seat to his mountain bike. It contained an extra tube and a small patch and tool kit. He also had a backpack that he'd wear. He'd packed light. First, he'd run his errands, then head to Grayson's. The homestead was nearly an hour by vehicle, and while he had no experience with walking it, he assumed it wouldn't take more than a day to ride there on a bicycle. He just hoped the tires held up.

He felt like a fool. For years, Grayson had warned to always keep his gas tank on full. But that was a pain in the ass. That meant stopping to fill up nearly every other day. *Who does that?*

Olivia had driven the girls to the beach and he was using Gabby's car. But it was nearly on empty, the red light shining bright. Not nearly enough gas to get to the farm. He could drive it as far as it'd take him, but he couldn't bring himself to abandon it on the side of the road—Gabby would wring his neck.

And his own everyday truck was at the dealership on an airbag recall. His other truck, an old '57 Chevy, was in Grayson's barn, ripped apart. If he could get it back together, he could fill up with the gas they stored behind the barn.

One more look over supplies and he'd take off. He wasn't looking forward to it. He'd barely ridden the bike since Gabby had brought it home, hoping he would use it as therapy for his leg. He and Gabby had been in a terrible car accident years ago. He'd been banged up pretty bad, Gabby had been shook up too, but worst of all, his mother-in-law had lost her life. Jake now carried the limp from the accident as a grim reminder of that dark night. Riding to the farm was going to be painfully slow—emphasis on the pain part.

He snapped a warm bottle of water into the holder, and hung Gabby's TSS ball cap from the handlebars. It had an attached mag light on the bill. He dug in the bag, his fingers pushing aside his wedding picture, three bottles of water and one Gatorade, six Cliff energy bars, a Lumens flash-light, two Bic lighters, a map in case his regular route was diverted, a bandana, a good knife, a small bottle of Monkey-Butt to help with the chafing from riding, a bundle of para-cord, a tarp, and a change of clothes, including several pairs of good, thick hiking socks, and a small first aid kit.

At the bottom, his fingers brushed the shammy-towel. He was careful not to unroll it. Within that towel, he'd hidden a Glock .40. He hoped he wouldn't have to use it, but if he did, at least thanks to his brother-in-law, he knew how—logistically anyway.

Grayson had been adamant that they all learn to shoot, and Jake was the worst shooter of the bunch. He'd lined up at the range beside Gabby, Olivia and Emma as Grayson played Range-master and Instructor and paced behind them. His wife, Gabby, was a crack-shot. Soon, they were calling her Annie Oakley. Her first day there she marked a tight grouping and sometimes dead-center hit on her targets.

Her little sister, Emma—who was married to a cop and got plenty of instruction on the side—did almost as well and felt very comfortable with a firearm. Emma's husband, Dusty, was beaming with pride for her.

When comparing targets, Grayson had teased him and said with more practice, he too could 'shoot like a girl.' Jake had thought he was being insulted until a few other guys at the range had made the same remark amongst each other. Apparently, women seemed to be natural shooters.

Except poor Olivia, Gabby's twin sister. Grayson had been thoroughly aggravated at his wife's inability to get comfortable with the gun and remember even the basic instructions. When he'd step behind her to give her a pointer, she'd frequently turn with the gun in her hand, aimed at Grayson. Jake had a hard time not laughing as he watched Grayson hit the floor, screaming "Don't muzzle me!" over and over again. Olivia would lift her ear protection to ask him what he said, only to be startled by the blast of the other shooter's firing, and Grayson yelling for her to *keep her ears on* while on the range. Olivia would get so flustered, she couldn't remember a thing.

Jake, Gabby and Emma would all laugh at their antics. They began calling them *The Honeymooners*. In reality, they kind of were. Married just shy of two years they were still feeling their way around each other. Dusty and Emma weren't married much longer; only three years. It was their wedding where Olivia had met Grayson, when he'd come in to stand up for his little brother as best man. He and Olivia had been caught in a hurricane on the island together, and fell in love, marrying exactly one year later in the same lighthouse that Emma and Dusty had married in.

After only one day on the range, Olivia had asked if Emma's husband, Dusty, could give her instructions instead. Jake wondered if it had stung Grayson's pride to be replaced by his little brother. But Olivia didn't do it out of malice—she'd never intentionally hurt Grayson's feelings —she'd just felt it would be safer and less stressful for Grayson if he wasn't trying to teach his own wife. Not to mention avoiding marital conflict.

As a police officer, and Grayson's younger brother, Dusty knew as much as Grayson did abut firearms, and was at least as good a shot. They'd trained together for years growing up and as adults. Dusty did work out to be the better instructor for Olivia than her husband was. He spent days on the range showing her the basics, and when she'd finally mastered loading, unloading, clearing misfires and a healthy grouping, he'd declared her trained, much to Olivia's relief—since she hated guns.

But Jake was glad they'd all gone through it. He knew the girls had their Get-Home bags with them. Grayson would've never let them leave home without them, and those bags had their guns and ammo. They might be needing some fire power, and he was glad that at least two out of the three could 'shoot like a girl.'

Jake walked around the bike for one more inspection. It was as good as it was going to get. He'd have to push it out the side door rather than wrestle with trying to manually open the garage door. He rolled it that way, but came to an abrupt stop when he saw Kenny, his neighbor, through the glass pane of the door. Red-faced and sweating, he looked to be in a panic.

"Jake! Come quick, there's a fight at Tucker's house!"

A fight? Shit. What was this, eighth grade?

Kenny ran away, toward Tucker's house and Jake hurried to get his bike out the door. He jumped on, pedaling as fast as his throbbing leg could manage. What did they want from him? He hoped it wasn't a stupid disagreement over some lame Home Owners Association—HOA—issue. That crap could wait. This wasn't the time for nitpicking over lawns, driveways, and dues. Times were about to get rough.

In normal times, *TullyMore*—the neighborhood—was already divisive. Half the residents followed the orders of the HOA, regardless of how ridiculous they were, and the other half blatantly ignored them or outright opposed them. The two sides had many small disagreements, as well as large disagreements; some ultimately resulting in nearly physical altercations. There had even been court battles over stupid things such as a camper being parked in a driveway.

Neighbors reported neighbors to the cops for noise. Walls were built. Feelings were hurt. Sides were chosen. At the worst of times, it felt like the Hatfield's & McCoy's.

But somehow, Jake and Gabby had managed to straddle the line and keep friends on both sides, maintaining a quiet and Switzerland-like sort of relationship with them all.

And now, here they were. Jake took a sharp turn into Tucker's driveway.

He saw people from *both* sides.

In a bloody brawl.

9

GRAYSIE

"Sir, I know we're not allowed to go to our cars. But I just need to get my backpack. See, these are my keys." Graysie held up her keys and jingled then, smiling innocently.

The security guard gave her a stern look. "Sorry, miss. I've got my instructions. I can't let you leave. It'd be my job on the line. We should know more about the situation in the next few days."

The university, supposedly on advice from the National Guard, had mandated all students temporarily stay in place if a parent didn't arrive to retrieve them. The cyberattack must have come from an enemy, and the government was waiting for the other shoe to drop. Would someone dare to attack us on our own soil? Or was the loss of all power enough of an attack for the assailant to just sit back and watch us die slowly as our world imploded around us? She'd be damned if she was going to lay around napping while the world fell apart. Dad always said no matter what happens, just come home. This would be one of the few times she would listen to him.

Graysie's shoulders fell and she let her head drop, causing her long, red hair to fall over her face. She shook her shoulders slightly and sniffled, followed by a low whimper.

The security guard took the bait. "Miss? Don't cry. I'm sorry. Look, what do you need so bad out of that bag? Maybe I can help you?"

Graysie used her best fake-crying-voice. "I doubt it, Mister. See, when young women are cramped up all close together like this, we tend to all start our... menses... together. There's not a feminine product to be found on my whole floor. Probably not on this floor either. And I have a lot of problems in that area, if you know what I mean. And now, there's no water to wash with either. But my step-mama made sure I was prepared. She and my daddy packed me a whole bag of girl-stuff and it's in my car. I just need that bag—quick."

She crossed her legs and leaned against the counter, taking a quick shuttered peek at her victim. As she thought he would, he looked flustered—and thoroughly grossed out. "The whole floor of ladies, you say? All having this same problem?"

"Yes sir, and I intend to share with them too." She took a swipe at her fake-tears before looking up through her long lashes at him. He quickly looked away. His face was turning red. She almost laughed. What was it with middle-aged dudes not being able to talk about a simple fact of life?

"I'll... um... I'm being relieved in thirty minutes. If you'll give me your keys, I'll get your bag and bring it to your room. Can you... um... wait that long?" he stuttered.

"Yes, sir. Thank you so much, sir. Here's where my car is parked." She pointed to a sticker on her key chain. "Mine is the red Mustang with a peace-sign on the back window. The bag's in the trunk. I'm in room 205. Last one at the end of the hall. I'll be waiting. We'll all be waiting. You're our hero," she said, and reached over the counter to give him a one-armed hug. She almost giggled when he cringed. *Dude, it's not contagious*, she thought as she ran up the stairs.

She burst in with a smile on her face, startling Becky from her sleep.

She rubbed her eyes and glared at Graysie. "What are you so happy about? Did something change?" she asked.

"Only that my dad really is going to help me get out of here and get home," she answered slyly. "I'm leaving within the hour."

10

GRAYSON

GRAYSON WAS GOING STIR crazy all alone out at the homestead. Finally, he'd thought about the gas in the lawnmower. And the gas in that old boat Jake had dragged out behind the barn. Between the two, he'd siphoned enough to go for a short ride in the truck.

He hurried into the house with Ozzie at his heels and washed the taste of gas out of his mouth, cringing at the pain of his bad tooth, and grabbed a T-shirt and a pair of khaki cargo shorts. He changed from his sweaty, dirty clothes, as he muttered to himself. "Been sweatin' like a two-dollar-whore on nickel night by myself out here. Be nice if someone could show up to help."

He slipped on a pair of shoes, grabbed his wallet and a leash and hurried out the door with Ozzie. "Come on, boy. Let's ride up the road and see if any neighbors are out. Maybe someone has some news about something." Grayson wouldn't say it out loud, but he hoped maybe his family was walking down the road right now. Not able to wait another minute, he hoped to meet them, although he couldn't go far on the limited gas he had.

Slowly, he rolled up the dirt road with his windows down. Living out in the country so spread apart, he rarely saw his neighbors in good times. But, maybe today would be his lucky day. He was embarrassed that he'd never exchanged much more than a wave when he had seen someone, but no time like the present to get to know each other.

The big house on the hill, a mile from his own older homestead, had a generator. Grayson could hear it buzzing at he drove by. The couple who lived there alone kept to themselves. The house was huge, with all the amenities, and their kids were grown. Grayson kept meaning to invite them over for dinner. He passed them on by. They weren't outside and he didn't know them well enough to knock on the door.

Yet.

Two horses grazed in their pasture surrounding the house as though they didn't have a care in the world. Ozzie gave a low whine.

"Envious boy? I forgot to feed you again, didn't I? Sorry." He ruffled his fur and Ozzie leaned into him, as usual quick to forgive. "I'll feed both of us as soon as we get back."

He drove slowly and turned at the next gravel road, passing two more small houses. No one outside and no signs of power there either.

At the stop sign, he took a left. Soon, he'd be coming up

on the backside of his own thirty acres. There was an old shack of a farmhouse somewhere along this road, not visible, other than the driveway. A woman and her grown son lived there, he'd been told. Rumor was they didn't have much of anything and relied on the government and church hand-outs. Their farm was overgrown now. He'd check on them and see if they'd heard anything yet.

He rolled to a stop next to the long dirt driveway and stuck his head out the window.

Three teenagers stood at the base of a huge tree, yelling and taunting something above them. Wearing hoodies in this beautiful weather only made them look like... well...*hood rats*. Baggy pants with cigarette pack shapes etched into their back pockets, and too-big high-top sneakers with the strings untied, they looked to be a wannabe bad crew. They gave him a passing glance and then went back at it, throwing rocks up into the tree and yelling, "Come down now or we're coming up to get ya."

Grayson could hear something caterwauling up there. A long keening sound shook him to his core. Whatever it was, it was terrified.

He didn't see a rifle anywhere.

What was it? Possibly a raccoon, but they usually only came out a night. Out here in the country, it could be a bobcat. Very dangerous. These boys might get more than they bargained for if they couldn't put it down when it finally landed.

Stupid kids.

Ozzie growled and tried to stick his head out too.

Grayson pushed him back and opened the door, stepping out with the dog jumping down behind him.

"What are you boys doing?" He walked over to the tree.

The boys whipped around, going into defensive stances.

Ozzie barked and gave a little lunge, startling all three of the skinny kids.

Grayson nearly laughed, and grabbed his collar, holding him back, but Ozzie had never bit a soul, and he doubted he'd start today. He was all bark and no bite.

Usually.

"What do you boys have treed up there?"

The supposedly toughest of the group, who were all probably only sixteen or seventeen, and a buck-thirty soaking wet, spit on the ground. "None of your business, mister. You need to move along."

The hair on the Ozzie's neck stood at attention and he growled at the boy's tone.

"It is my business. You're pretty close to my property line. If you boys have treed a wildcat or something up there, and it comes down and hurts you, I could be liable. You don't even have a gun. You need to get on home. You don't live around here, do you?" Grayson had never seen these teenagers before. They didn't look much like the typical country-boy teenagers around these parts. The outfits were all wrong.

Ball-caps, Levis and shit-kickers were the style around here.

The boy moved lightning quick and reached into the front of his baggy pants, pulling out a pistol and aiming it at

Grayson gangster-style; sideways. "We *got* guns. *You* need to get on home, old man," he snarled while bobbing his head side to side.

The other two boys hooted and hollered, encouraging him. Grayson noticed neither of the other two pulled out a weapon though. Normally an old man comment wouldn't have riled Grayson up, seeing as he was hitting forty on his next birthday and already showing gray throughout his mustache and goatee, but today, it pissed him off.

It hadn't been a good couple of days.

Definitely not a good day to have a gun pulled on him.

Ozzie went nuts; snarling and pulling at his collar. He didn't like anything pointed at his people. Grayson gave him a jerk back. "Stay, Ozzie."

"Yeah, you better stay, dog. Or you'll be leaking like a sieve." The boy bobbed his head left to right when he spoke, then looked to his crew for appreciation. "Am I right?"

They acknowledged him with bitter laughs and high fives.

The kid went too far, talking smack to Olivia's dog.

Grayson sucked in his breath and held it a moment while he grit his teeth.

Didn't help.

He covered the space between them in three stomps, shoving one hand into the kid's chest and pushing him back while jerking the gun away from him with his other hand. He gave the kid a light smack on the side of the head with the butt of the gun before stepping back.

"Next time you pull on someone, you might want to turn the fucking safety off, hotshot. And here's another piece of advice for you. If you don't have a holster, at least carry the gun in the *back* of your pants. You'd rather have another hole in your ass than shoot your little pecker off, am *I* right?" he asked sarcastically, bobbing his own head left to right in his impression of the kid.

The boy gasped and grabbed his head and then looked at his hand.

Wasn't a drop of blood, but a bump would surely rise.

He was furious. "Give it back!"

Grayson shook his head and smiled. "I'll give it back to your daddy. Where you live, boy?"

His friends stepped back a few paces, and then took off at a fast run. One of them yelled over his shoulder, "Come on, Darion! Run!"

Darion took one look at his posse abandoning him, and then sneered at Grayson. "I know where you live. I'll get my gun back, old man," he threatened.

Grayson shrugged. "Bring your daddy, Cupcake. Otherwise I might have to give you another spankin'."

Darion shot him the bird and ran.

Grayson stuck the gun in the back of his own shorts and leaned into the tree, looking up.

I'll be damned.

It wasn't an animal. It was another kid. This one looked older than the group that had run off—and younger, at the same time.

"Hey, you can come down now, they're gone."

He whimpered and hid his tear-stained face against the tree.

"Come on, I'm not going to hurt you. Get down from there."

Ozzie whimpered too.

The kid stole a peek at the dog. "That dog gonna bite me, mister?" he asked in a child-like voice. "I'm afraid. He has big teeth."

Grayson's raised an eyebrow. *Is he kidding me? What's with the baby talk?*

"Naw, he's friendly to friendlies. Come down and I'll let you pet him. Ozzie's like a big teddy bear. Watch this." He pointed his finger at Ozzie like a gun. "Bang bang!"

Ozzie fell over onto his back with his four feet in the air. He slung his head to the side and let his tongue hang out. *The big ham.*

A child-like giggle came from the tree, and then the kid threw down a sack. A few garden vegetables rolled out of it. He followed, scaling the tree as fast as a monkey. A *big* monkey. He jumped to the ground and stood back staring at Ozzie, his hand over his mouth in wonder.

Grayson was a bit astonished too. This wasn't just kid. He was a *man*. A man-child? At least twenty years old and built like an ox. Grayson wasn't a short man, but even at his six foot one inch height, he had to look up at the boy. His face was childlike, but covered in a thin sheen of pale blonde, almost white, baby-fine whiskers. His hair was the same color. Tow-headed. His features were...exaggerated. Something about him looked odd.

"What's your name, kid?"

"Fuckin' Puck."

Grayson raised his eyebrows. "No need to cuss me, son."

"I'm not trying to, mister. Mama Dee would whoop me," he replied innocently and looked toward the ground, losing eye contact with Grayson.

"You said 'fucking.' That's a curse word where I come from."

"But you asked my name."

Grayson squeezed his eyes in confusion. *Okay, one more time...* "What's your name?"

"Fuckin' Puck."

Grayson laughed. "Is that what your Mama Dee calls you?"

The kid looked up, but didn't crack a smile. "No, that's what my daddy called me. But he's dead. Mama Dee just calls me Puck. Have you seen her?" His eyes were wide and hopeful.

"Your mama?"

"Yessir."

"No, I can't say that I have, son."

"She was s'posed to be home," he held his hand up and slowly lifted his fingers one at a time until two fingers were up as though he were giving the peace sign, "two sleeps ago. But she's not. I was all by myself. My nightlight won't work. Do you think she'll be home before tonight, mister?"

Something was wrong with this kid. His cornbread wasn't all the way done in the middle or something. He sounded like a five-year old but looked like a gorilla. "I don't know, Puck," Grayson wasn't about to call him *Fucking Puck.* "Where did she go?"

"She went to Lumby to get our boxes. She goes every month but she always comes back the same day. Sometimes she gets home real late. I get something special for staying home."

"Lumby?"

"The big town across the bridges. Mama Dee makes me stay home cuz I'm scared of the bridges and I track her when she's driving."

Track her?

Distract maybe?

"Columbia?" Not that there was a huge bridge or anything on the way to Columbia, but the interstate had plenty of bridge overpasses and there were small bridges covering creeks and lows. If the power was out in Columbia too, she might've got caught with no gas to get home. It was a little over an hour away—same city Graysie attended college.

"There's no one to stay with you?"

"Jenny, but she likes to sleep in the barn. This stuff is for her." He bent down and scooped up the vegetables, awkwardly stuffing them back into the bag.

That was odd, but Graysie had slept in the barn before. Usually, only when she had a friend over though, and most of the time, they'd end up back in the house before morning with tales of bugs, rats and scary things that went bump in the night. Girls didn't typically like to sleep in barns.

"Is Jenny your sister?"

"No. But Mama Dee says we're about the same age. Mama Dee says we're all like family."

Was Jenny the same...er...intelligence as Puck? If she was, these kids shouldn't be left alone. If Olivia was there, she'd insist on taking care of them until their mother returned.

"Do you and Jenny want to come stay with me until your mama gets home?"

Puck dragged his enormous boot through the dirt and looked down. He whistled with his head hung low, seeming to forget Grayson and Ozzie were even there. Soon he tugged his too-big britches up until his ankles were showing, paying no mind to Grayson or his question.

Grayson ducked his head down and looked up into Puck's face. "It's okay. I have a girl about your age myself. She's away at college right now though. You can trust me."

Puck frantically shook his head. "Mama Dee wouldn't like that. And Jenny doesn't like strangers. I need to stay home."

"I could meet her. Then I wouldn't be a stranger, right? My name's Grayson, by the way." He stuck his hand out in greeting, only for it to hang there empty.

Puck shrugged and screwed up his lips, looking away. He was obviously avoiding the suggestion to meet Jenny, and the handshake. Then, as though just remembering, he exclaimed, "She's hungry. Mama Dee was bringing Jenny some food too. Spose'd to anyway."

Jenny wasn't the only one hungry. He could hear Puck's

stomach growling. He doubted the boy could cook, and apparently neither could Jenny. "Why were you up in that tree?"

"I like trees. People don't see me up there. Usually. I was looking for Mama Dee cuz I can see far up there. But the mean boys," Puck's lip quivered. "They wanted Jenny's food."

"Where'd you get that food?"

"I borrowed it. Jenny's hungry."

Grayson scratched his head, still surprised at the child-like responses coming from the young man. No wonder the boys were chasing him. He was worried about them coming back too, even though apparently Puck was the thief. Did they know Puck lived right down that dirt road next to where they were standing?

"Listen, kid. You can't take things that don't belong to you. That's stealing."

Puck hung his head and Grayson realized he was crying again.

Oh hell.

Grayson reached out and patted Puck's back, only to be surprised at the kid flinching. He stepped back to give him some room. "Hey now. It's okay. But don't do it again, huh? How about you ride over to the house with me, and I'll cook you and Jenny some hamburgers on the grill. Something to hold you over until your mama gets home."

Puck pursed his lips and looked up at the sky. He swiped the tears off his cheeks. Finally, he answered, "I'd really like that. Do you have a pickle? Mama Dee gives me a pickle with my burger. But I'm not s'posed to be talking to strangers. Or going to someone's house."

He looked back up into the sky, leaving his mouth hanging open a moment. Then suddenly blurted out, "Maybe I can just stay outside so Mama Dee don't get mad? Jenny won't eat a burger. So just for me."

"She doesn't like *hamburgers*? How about a hot dog then?"

"No meat. Meat makes Jenny throw up." Puck beamed as though he'd answered a million-dollar trivia question. He held up the sack of salad stuff like a trophy, seemingly not ashamed of his theft after all. "This is for her."

"Meat makes her sick? Is she pregnant?"

Puck squeezed his eyebrows together and shrugged.

"Is she going to have a baby?" Grayson further explained.

Puck screwed up his face in disgust. "I don't think so."

Jenny sounded like a heap of trouble. Probably one of those millennial vegetarians or something. Graysie had brought a friend home a month ago that said she was 'vegan,' and had nearly drove him and Olivia both up a wall. Their family was big on meat. But Grayson felt sure he could come up with something more filling than a salad.

"Come on, then. Get in the truck. I'll make you both something."

Puck hooted and hollered and ran to the truck, jumping in the back in a single leap, into the truck bed where he sat against the cab and grabbed the side. He tightly held on and yelled, "Ready, Mister Gray Man." He squeezed his eyes shut and grinned, as though about to take off on a carnival ride.

Grayson sighed and smiled. This kid was weird. *Mr. Gray Man?* He ran his hand over his mustache and goatee. Maybe it was time to let Graysie get creative with some hair dye. And riding in the back wasn't exactly safe—or legal —nowadays.

Hell, it was only a few miles home, he could ride in the back. Why not? What's the worst that could happen in two miles?

11

THE LADIES

GABBY GLARED at Olivia in disbelief, her eyes nearly bugging out of her head.

"Are you serious? You left your bag *at home*? What were you thinking? Did Grayson know you were leaving it? I thought he'd told all of us to never, ever leave without it? So, you're exempt, because, why?"

Olivia raised her shoulders up around her ears, and closed her eyes. "I know. I'm an idiot. I swear, this is the *only* time I've ever taken it out of my car. Grayson has no idea. But I didn't have room for all of our luggage, and three more bags. I threw mine and Emma's out in the garage when you guys were in the house. And... I hit my head," she whined, hoping to use her injury again against Gabby's wrath.

"Emma's too?" Gabby shook her head. "And the bleeding stopped. You'll live. We'll work on it in the car— with *my* first aid kit from *my* bag. This really makes me mad, Olivia. You should know the one time you *leave* it, Murphy's Law, is the one time you *need* it. I can't believe you left both of them. *Seriously*?"

Emma calmly stepped between her older sisters. "Hey, what's done is done. We've still got one. We'll be fine. Besides, we're not walking. Home is only four hours away, maybe a little more with all the stalled cars on the road. But as long as we're riding, we shouldn't even need the bags. There's not time to fight now, we need to get to Larry's car before he changes his mind and leaves us."

Gabby sucked in a breath and held it for a moment, willing herself to calm down. Emma was right, there was no use being mad at Olivia. They couldn't change the fact that they now had only one bag with *one gun*. And a small bag at that. She didn't know what was in it, but couldn't be much. They'd just have to make do with what they had. They were probably luckier than most of the people in this tourist town, she doubted many carried a Get-Home bag at all. Now they just needed a way to carry all this other stuff. Emma and Olivia could each hold a bag on their lap, if they had one. She studied the huge pile on the bed.

"Emma, you sort this stuff. We can't take it all. We need the water, the phones, one hat each, one clean shirt each, a pair of socks each—pack three pair even though Olivia doesn't have shoes—and any jewelry or valuables we have here. Also, get our wallets, my Chap Stick, and sunglasses for all of us. Roll the clothes tight to make more room. Olivia, you need to take real sneakers, not flip-flops. *Hurry.* I'll make us a something to carry it all in."

If only they could have a do-over. In a situation like this *may* be, they needed all their guns. She wished they'd listened to Grayson and started carrying concealed on their person or in their purses. And she wished they'd all brought sturdier pants; a pair of jeans at least. All they had were shorts, dresses and bikinis.

Olivia cringed. "I didn't bring any sneakers. All I have are flip-flops and sandals."

Omigod. This can't get any worse. Gabby ran her hands over her face and shook her head. Ignoring Olivia, she snatched the scissors out of her make-up case and grabbed the largest T-shirt in the pile. Probably a workout shirt, or sleep-shirt.

She laid it flat on the other bed and cut off the sleeves, going in further than the seam, turning the T-shirt into a tank-top. She cut the collar out of the middle, making it more of a deep scoop-neck-tee, turned it inside-out and cut thin strips four to five inches long across the bottom of the shirt, fringing it, and finally tied the knots together, two at a time. She finished the entire row across the bottom of the shirt, and then started from the other side tying knots again to the knot next to it until the bottom was double-secure. She flipped the shirt right-side out and held it up.

"A tote-bag! Where'd you learn to do that?" Emma grabbed it and shoved as much of the new pile that would fit into it. The newly-cut shoulder straps made perfect handles.

"Pinterest." Gabby hurried to make one more, finishing

in minutes and stuffing it with the rest of the pile. "Now come on, we've got to go!"

The girls rushed out of the room, looking over their shoulders at all they were leaving behind. All their stuff; sandals, clothes, books, hair products and equipment, three little black dresses hanging in the tiny open closet, bought for a night out; and most of it was new, bought just for this trip. It was painful to leave it. As Gabby looked at the scattered strappy heels and wedged sandals slung across the floor, she wished she'd brought an extra pair of sneakers for Olivia.

And Olivia would wish she had as well, before it was all over.

12

JAKE

JAKE JUMPED off his bike and into the fray—into a blur of fists and elbows flying.

He couldn't make out who was fighting who, or who was trying to break up the fight. It was a bloody, sweaty pack of middle-aged, angry men.

Wives were screaming. Kids were backed up against the brick drive-way wall, quivering in fear at seeing their daddies fight. Babies were crying. It was mayhem and chaos.

Normally, he was a laid-back guy, but under the circumstances, he threw his own weight into pulling the guys off one-by-one and slinging them onto the ground. With the help of Kenny—who really wasn't much help at all—and a few of the other neighbors who until Jake arrived had been standing back out of the fight, he managed to break it up.

"What...the hell...is going on?" he yelled at the crowd, huffing and puffing through his words.

Tucker may have been the nicest guy there, but he was probably the one guy in the 'hood that Jake wouldn't ever want to go up against. He was lean and ripped with muscles and heavy into mixed martial arts, having several black belts in some type of Kung Fu stuff. Right now, he was spittin' mad. He swiped his arm across his red, sweaty face and stared daggers at Curt, the HOA president.

Seeing Tucker angry was a rare sight. Tucker was a happy-go-lucky sort of guy who was the life of Tullymore. He and his wife, Katie, hosted most of the neighborhood functions, since the HOA couldn't pull their heads out of their asses and organize anything. Katie was a phenomenal cook and a good friend to nearly everyone. The couple was very well-liked. But Tucker and Curt were sworn enemies; they just both rubbed each other wrong, no matter what the situation.

Tucker pointed at Curt. "This asshole thinks he's the king of this subdivision. He came to get water out of my pool, without asking, and brought all his friends." Tucker's face was blood-red. The ones willing to go up against Tucker in this fight were probably regretting it about now. Curt huddled on the ground cradling one arm. Other guys, the typical HOA crowd, all stood bleeding and hurt, too.

Jake almost smirked. Good thing he and Tucker were friends.

He shook his head. "Y'all need to go on home now. It's only been a few days. I don't know why you think it's okay to come on someone's property and take *anything*, but it's not. Things aren't that bad, and I hope they never are. Besides that, we've been without power a few days before, so I don't know why y'all are losing your minds over it."

He picked his bike up and threw a leg over.

"Wait, Jake," Curt, the HOA president yelled. "Where are you going?"

He bristled at being questioned by Curt. He didn't owe these people an explanation and resented being put on the spot. "I'm going to pick up a part for my truck," he answered anyway, always needing to keep the peace.

Curt dragged himself to his feet and puffed his chest up. Short and squatty, with his face so red, he looked like a fire plug. "The power's been out a few days before, but never the cell service and internet *and* the power, all at the same time. We can't get any real news from anywhere. We're cut off from everything. But CNN talked about cyber-attacks *the night before* the lights went out and other stations have been talking about it since *before* the election. Your president has provoked China, Russia, Korea and just about every other country. I think this is war."

Curt just had to get his stab in at Trixler.

"No, *our* president just isn't taking shit from anyone anymore. He's making America great again!" someone in the crowd yelled out.

The group began to scream at each other again. Several ladies were silently crying. So this is what had been talked about in the few days he'd been holed up at home. They were probably right about this being different. Jake couldn't remember a time all three services were knocked out at once. The world had been slowly going crazy. Maybe this *was* the big event Grayson had warned about.

"That doesn't mean all hell has to break loose here."

Curt continued, "All hell has broken loose *everywhere*. Some of us have been to town. There's no more gas, no more food, and people have lost their minds, shooting at each other over the last of everything. It's not safe to leave the neighborhood, even if we could."

"Then stay here and stop fighting. Wait for it to all blow over," Jake suggested. "It's not the end of the world. At least I don't think it is..." He pushed his bike further up the driveway, hoping to get away. The last thing Jake needed was more drama.

Kenny, his annoying next-door neighbor, waved a hand at the crowd behind him. "Wait. You live here too. Before you leave, can you vote or something? We need to settle this now."

"Vote on what?"

Kenny, normally a passive, but at times whiny guy, glanced at Tucker worriedly before answering. "The swimming pools. There's a lot of us nearly out of water, but there's two pools in the subdivision. Curt says these people should share it with everyone else."

The crowd came alive with comments, and mumblings, soon erupting into outbursts. At this rate, they'd be swinging fists again.

It was all too much. He couldn't care less about the

damn water. His head was throbbing, and in spite of the beautiful weather, he was breaking out in a cold sweat. "Hey!" he screamed. "Y'all shut up!"

That shocked the crowd. No one had ever heard or seen Jake get riled up, which was why they sent Kenny to get him at the first sign of trouble. He was always one of the most level-headed in the neighborhood—not to mention he didn't really belong to either side of the constantly-fighting divisions. Jake had earned everyone's respect with his normally quiet demeanor and willingness to always help out a neighbor, and not pick a side.

"It doesn't make a difference to me. I'm not taking sides, if that's what y'all are asking me to do. Work it out."

Tucker stepped up to speak quietly to Jake. "Hey, Jake, wait a minute. Look, we need you man. These people here don't have a clue what to do in a situation like this and tempers are flaring. We need to work together, but you know Curt's not going to listen to a word I have to say. I don't mind sharing our water, but not like this. I'm not having him in charge. He's clueless. You've been doing this prepping stuff with your family—we've talked about it. So, you know more than probably anyone. Can you spare a few minutes to just get us started? People will listen to you."

Jake sighed. Tucker rarely asked Jake for anything. As far as Jake knew, Tucker and his family had nowhere else to go, they were transplants here. Their family was out of state. If the power didn't come back on—if this truly was a shit hit the fan event—he'd feel awful leaving Tucker and

Katie and the kids behind anyway. The least he could do was give them his two cents.

Still, he didn't want to get involved. He needed to run his errands and get on the road to the farm. The longer he waited, the worse his leg was going to be hurting him, and it was going to be a long ride. He slowly shook his head. He wasn't sticking around.

Tucker put his hand on Jake's shoulder. "Look, I saw you limping. You really going to ride that bike all the way to town to get your part? You'll be miserable. You won't make it there and back before dark tonight."

Jake nodded miserably. "I know."

"I'll make you a deal. If you stick around a little while— an hour at the most—and help me herd these cats, I'll let you borrow my four-wheeler ATV to go get your part."

Oh hell yeah.

Jake was in. He needed more than a part, but both stops were near each other. He really didn't want to pedal that far. "You talked me into it."

He stepped off his bike and faced the crowd, crossing his arms. "Okay, what all have y'all done so far? Assuming the power isn't coming on for a while. Have you stocked up the water and cooked all your food?"

Nothing but blank stares answered him.

He nodded and did some quick thinking through the waves of his worsening headache. He wasn't up for a nasty debate, as their neighborhood meetings usually devolved into. He'd give them the quick and dirty version and then be on his way.

"First thing, leave Tucker's pool alone. Y'all got more water than you think you do at your own houses. Maybe even enough to last until the power comes back on. So, if you haven't already done it, drain your pipes. Use any pot or pan or container you have and fill them up. There's somewhere around sixty houses in Tullymore, right? With sixty, having at least one water heater each that can be drained, that's a fifty-gallon heater x 60 houses = 3,000 gallons of available drinking water. The city has already treated it with chemicals in their process, so it should stay good for a pretty long while. The main supply lines from under the houses can also be taken loose and all the water sitting in the lines throughout the house could be caught in buckets, jars, bottles or anything that will hold it. I would have to think that there would be at least four or five more gallons in a typical house in just the pipes alone. Be careful with it. If the power doesn't come back on, you're going to need every drop. When you're done with all that, turn off the main water and sewer connections at the street."

Paul, the neighborhood lawyer, yelled over the crowd, "Why would we do that? We won't know when it's on then, and we'll just have to turn it back on again when the power comes back on."

Jake could see no one else knew where he was going with this. He gave an internal sigh—at least he hoped it was internal—at the lack of basic understanding of how city waste and water worked. "If you don't turn it off at the road, when the pipes at the water plant clog up because the shit-choppers stop chopping, all that shitty water is gonna reverse and come back this way. Your toilets, your sinks, your tubs... will all be overflowing with sewage. Soon, you won't be able to live with the stink, assuming you could stop the waves of waste flowing across your floors. Just turn them off."

He looked back over the crowd for any further arguments. That's what he thought. Everyone was a big man until faced with shit. Literally.

"Once your lines are shut down, you can't use your toilets, not even if you add your own water. So, you'll need to dig your own hole in the ground and make an outhouse. Get a five-gallon bucket and cut the bottom out, put it over the hole. You can probably take your toilet seat off and use it on the bucket rim for comfort. Or you could also use cutdown pool noodles, the Styrofoam floatie-kind, if you have them.

But if the power stays out too long, I'd suggest a community latrine—actually two. One for the ladies, and one for the men. Dig a long, narrow, ditch-like pit, maybe twenty feet long. If you want to make it comfortable for those that aren't used to squatting, then find some two by four lumber and build a sturdy narrow bench over it. Hang a coffee can on a tree or a post to keep your toilet paper dry and bugs out of it. Lots of people around here probably have lime for their yards; you can sprinkle that over the sh —er—waste, when it gets too smelly. You can nail or staple some sheets or something up for a privacy screen. If you don't have lime, you can sprinkle the ashes from a fireplace, or fire pit on it to help with the smell—and the flies."

Curt, the HOA president, nudged the HOA secretary, Christie. "You getting all this?"

She nodded as she continued to furiously scribble on a notepad.

Jake had their full attention now. Most of this was common sense and he felt sure there was someone in this community who knew all this and much more. They just hadn't spoke up yet.

"I'm not saying this is gonna last a long while, but like my brother-in-law says, better to be prepared. With that in mind, don't put your latrines near any gardens anyone might have, or might put in the future. Make sure the latrine is downhill from the gardens, or potential garden spots, and especially from any water source, if you find one."

He doubted that would happen. He wasn't aware of any creek or pond nearby.

"You need to start rationing water and food now. This neighborhood has enough people in it to either trade with each other, or simply band together and work as one big team. We have a doctor here. You never know when you or families may need one. Put him in charge of health and accidents. Pitch in to give him some supplies. I doubt the hospitals are open."

Jake looked around at the crowd, trying to remember what everyone else did for a living. He felt confident there were skills here that could help, but he just couldn't remember them right now. If this kept on though, they'd discover who could do what eventually. Until then, everyone just needed to pitch in.

"You've got strong men and boys. Some can do the latrine digging and someone's gonna have to re-cover them up when they get too full and dig another. Going to need a lot of cooks for this many people, too, if you band together as a community, which I think you should if the power is not on in a week.

If that happens, y'all need to designate one family that you trust to hold and inventory all the food. Someone else can work with them to plan meals for the community. Help each other. Form teams. Food team to cook. Laundry team. Firewood chopping team. Water treatment and carry team —you can use pool shock or chlorine to treat water for drinking or cooking with. Or Bleach. Or you can boil it.

If you all work together and share the food and water, I'd make it a rule that if you don't work, you don't eat. Because you're going to find there's work to do *all* the time. Unless you're physically unable to work at all. And the doctor needs to be the final word on that. I think most everyone can do something, though. Also, one of the most important things that needs to be done right now is to designate a security team. If all hell is breaking loose in town, it'll be coming this way soon. Y'all asked for my opinion and I'm going to tell you, Tucker is your guy for that. Not only is he a martial arts specialist, but he's smart, he knows how to shoot and fight, and he has his own guns. Let him pick his own team. Let him train them. If you want to keep what food you have, and keep this community safe, then give all your guns and ammo to the team to protect you.

If the power comes back on, everyone agrees to give it all back and go back to their regular lives. I truly hope it goes that way soon. Until then, maybe put someone in charge of all the teams. Or put together a board to share that responsibility, a small group that can vote on big issues."

Curt stepped up in front of the crowd. "As the HOA president, I'll be in charge. I'll be sending the secretary and a team of a few people with carts to collect all the food to bring to one location."

The group went wild and tempers flared again.

Jake cleared his throat and waved them silent. "With all due respect, Curt. This isn't an HOA situation. This is a *real-life* situation. If you're put in charge, I think you should be voted into that position fairly. In a democratic way. Every house gets one vote."

Curt grit his teeth and glared at first Jake, and then Tucker. "Look how that worked out for our country, huh?"

Tucker tried to hide a grin. Curt hated President Trixler, and several of the guys had tortured him by sneaking *Trixler for President* signs in his yard at night for a solid year before Trixler was elected. Jake had been a part of it; all in good fun.

Someone in the crowd yelled out, "I think Jake should be in charge."

Several people audibly agreed.

Jake shook his head. "Thank you, but I can't. My wife

isn't home. She's out of town. When she comes home, she'll be going to her sister's house first. That's where I'm headed later. I may be back soon, but I don't want that responsibility. There's people here who are probably more than qualified to manage everything. I'd suggest you all sit down and decide what teams you need. Then take volunteers. Have the volunteers sign up and list any experience they have. If you've got a stay-at-home mom who's volunteered in the school cafeteria, or maybe even a caterer, they've got experience cooking for crowds. And someone here might be over inventory at their company. They'd be your food and supply manager. Any law enforcement here? Retired military? They'd be an asset to the security team. Use your assets."

"Any other advice?" Tucker asked.

Jake looked up into the air, thinking. "Empty your freezers and refrigerators now. First thing. Cook all the meat before it goes bad. You can cook it on the grill or over a fire, or some people might have camp-stoves. Cook it to eat just what you need. For the rest, you can smoke it, or dehydrate it to make jerky that will keep longer. You can also salt the pork and fish if you have enough salt—that'll keep your meat good for a really long time, and don't forget to use the salt you have on hand from your water softener systems."

He looked around the group for the few elderly couples that lived there. They didn't socialize much but they were old enough that they might know a few things about long-term food preparation from watching their parents or grandparents.

"There's hunters in here, and elderly, which probably know how to salt meat for keeping long-term. Salt as much as you can to save it in case of hard times. Ration it. If you have vegetables that are going to go bad, collect all the canning jars you can find from the neighborhood. You'll need lids and rings too. The meat can also be canned but it needs to be pressure-canned. If you have someone who knows how to safely 'can' the food for long-term storage, you can put all that up for later, just in case. Try to save the seeds from your veggies and produce if they're heirloom to plant for more food. No one knows how long this will last. If you're not sure what seeds to save, save them all. Nominate a garden specialist and have them take a look at what you got.

If this keeps on, pick one good community gathering spot. Somewhere that has shade and plenty of space, and maybe near one of the swimming pools. Drag as many tables and chairs there as you can. Make it your community center. You'll probably need three fires going all the time. Have someone rig some racks to hang the pots. One fire to constantly boil water for cooking and drinking. One fire for actually cooking over, and one fire for a laundry pot or hot water for sponge-baths for the kids."

A moan rolled through the crowd as people realized showers or full baths with hot water would be rare and a good bit of trouble for the near future.

Jake was tapped out. He couldn't think of anything else to suggest.

"I've got to roll. I want to see my wife, and I aim to be there before she is. I wish you all luck and please, don't fight each other anymore. Act like grown-ups, at least in front of the kids."

The next ten minutes was filled with the families that considered Jake and Gabby friends saying good bye and good luck to him. Soon, several people had sat down in a large circle, surrounded by the other neighbors standing behind them, and were writing down ideas that were being thrown at them for the different teams. Everyone seemed to be getting along fine.

So far.

Jake was ready to go.

Tucker shook his hand. "Thanks, man. That was really helpful. I think we just needed someone everyone would listen to, to settle things down and get us started with a plan. I know there's a lot of people who know this stuff but they're afraid to speak up, or if they do speak up, Curt is going to argue with them. I'm glad you put him in his place."

Jake shrugged. "I wasn't trying to do that. I was just stating a fact. This isn't HOA business. First step for y'all is going to be to nominate someone to be in charge and vote on that. After that, everything's on that guy. Or lady. Or board, I guess. Now, can I get that four-wheeler?"

Jake grabbed his bag off the bike, and they walked as quickly as Jake could manage to Tucker's second garage at the back of his lot. On the way there, Tucker told Jake what all he and his family had on hand. It was plenty to last a few weeks, maybe a month.

The way he was talking, Jake wasn't sure he would share with the neighborhood. Why should he? Some people probably had nothing. But Jake was leaving that up to them. He'd done his part, they could work out the details from here.

When they reached the garage, Tucker's wife, Katie, came out and gave Jake a big hug and told him to give one to Gabby for her. They stepped in, and Jake was surprised to see their kids, all at some level of teen or tween, sorting food into small meal groups and writing stuff down. They laughed at a joke Jake had missed, picking at one another. There were two boys, and two girls. Tucker had a houseful. And it was always a happy house. Jake smiled at the sibling camaraderie.

"How soon you need this back? It'd be great if you let me drive it to the homestead, too."

Tucker didn't seem very happy about that and hesitated to answer.

"Wait, how 'bout this?" Jake dug in his pocket and pulled out his house keys. He handed them to Tucker. "If you trust me with your four-wheeler, I'll trust you with my house. If I'm not back here in one week, with your four-wheeler intact, you and Katie are welcome to any food or supplies you find at our house. Is that fair?"

Tucker shook his head. "Naw, man. We're not gonna take your stuff. You'll get it back to me. My family is here, safe with me. I'm happy to help you get to yours." Tucker nodded firmly and tried to give Jake his keys back.

Jake refused to take the keys and instead started up the four-wheeler. "Hang onto those for me. The offer stands. At the very least, sneak in when no one is looking and get the freezer foods later today. I haven't opened the door at all, some of it'll still be good if you do it right away. No use in wasting it."

He stuck out his hand and Tucker grasped it firmly, and then pulled Jake into a one-armed hug. "You take care of yourself, Jake. Thanks again for getting us started, and if you can come back and help me herd these cats, please do."

Jake quickly returned the hug with a pat on Tucker's back, and pulled back. "You take care of Katie and the kids —and my bike—and keep the cats of Tullymore safe. I'll see ya later."

"Hey, you got a gun?"

"Yeah, got one in my bag right here."

"How 'bout you carry it on you. Things are already bad, man."

Jake dug through the bag and found the gun. He carefully stuck it behind him in his waistband and pulled his shirt over it, but not before Tucker saw his stomach.

"Looks like you maybe you *do* need to ride that bike. Got a few extra pounds there, buddy."

Tucker was full of shit. While he *was* in much better shape, Jake was no slouch. They worked out together every few weeks and Tucker was constantly badgering him to do more, just to heckle him.

"You worry about your own girlish figure," Jake answered, and laughed. He hopped on the 4-wheeler and threw a hand up behind him, giving a quick wave goodbye.

But if he'd had known then the shape Tucker would be in when they next met, he'd have held that last hug with his friend a bit longer and tighter.

GRAYSIE HUDDLED on her bed and opened the backpack her father had packed for her. The security guard had practically thrown it at her in his hurry to get away from the horrifying wave of menstruating young women.

Her roommate, Becky, had disappeared again, luckily before the guard had brought her bag. She was glad to have the privacy. Whatever she found, she wasn't sharing with Becky.

The first thing she saw was an envelope with her name written in cursive across the front. She pulled out the two-page letter, and seeing it was also written in cursive, she leaned back on her pillows to read. Seeing her father's handwriting—they called it their secret code, as schools had stopped teaching it and most of her friends couldn't read or write cursive—squeezed her heart. She felt a lump building in her throat. She wished he could swoop in and take her home. They'd argued for so long about her not wanting to spend her weekends at the farm. She'd wanted to stay in Columbia, with her friends as much as she could. Now she wished she could take it all back. She'd give anything to be at the farm right this minute.

The letter read:

Graysie,

If you're reading this letter, one of two things have happened. Either 1) You've been partying all night and have the munchies, and you are looking for a quick snack, or 2) You're in a serious situation and you need to get home. If it is number one, I'd ask that just this once, you listen to your stupid 'ole dad and put this letter away, close the bag, and put it back in your car. Don't even peek. There's nothing in here you need right now, but everything that you might really need later. Please, do as I ask, this one time without question. Put it away.

If it's number two, flip the page and read on.

Graysie turned the paper over.

Okay, so you're in a situation. I'm glad you remembered the bag. If you're still reading, I'm assuming you're at college, or somewhere else away from home. Your number one priority is to get home. Hear me? Get home, quick. You can do this. You're a strong girl, you have your mother's stubborn Irish streak to go along with those red curls and green eyes. I can't say enough how sorry I am that we lost your mother at Hurricane Katrina. Even though I have Olivia now, my heart still bleeds for your mom. I loved—still love—her very much. She was your mom... but she was my wife.

I imagine you're getting angry now, as you do each time I bring her up. I wish you'd let it go. It is true, I could've saved her, but I would have lost you. It was her wish that I went for you first. You won't let me talk about this to you, and I don't know if you truly remember, but you'd already gone under twice. I was closer to your mom, but you were in the most trouble. She begged me to go to you. I did it for both of us. I tried to get back to her after I had you to safety, but she was already gone. I followed her wishes, and I truly feel that now she's watching over you. Watching over both of us. The things I've done at the farm, to be prepared for any other disaster, are for you. I won't let you down again. But first things first, I need you here, where I can take care of you.

Graysie swiped at her wet eyes. It was true. She had blamed her dad for not saving their mom. She'd couldn't remember much of anything from that fateful day, but she'd been forced to listen to the story repeatedly. She knew he could only save one of them.

She swallowed hard and vowed to finally let it go and stop holding it against him. He was her father. He did the best he could, and losing mom was just as hard on him as it was on her. She'd been a real ass to him.

The three most important things you'll need are water, food, and protection. I've taken care of the first two in this bag. The third thing can be found in your dorm. (I hope you're in your dorm when you read this) You'll be surprised to know when I was putting your bed together I did more than turn some screws. Lay down on the floor and crawl underneath your bed. Look in the far, far corner. Be careful with what you find!

Graysie threw the letter down and jumped to the floor, lying on her stomach and scooting under. She pushed aside bins of shoes and several old notebooks and looked at the bottom of the mattress.

There.

A box wrapped in brown paper.

She grabbed it and scooted out, sitting up to look at it.

The box said 'Grade-School: Awards, Ribbons & Mementos.' Graysie scrunched her eyebrows together. What the heck did she want with those? Did her dad think her childhood accomplishments would inspire and encourage her to get home? *What the heck, Dad?*

She ripped the paper off anyway. When she lifted the lid, her eyes widened. It was her dad's favorite pistol—a Smith & Wesson .38 Special—and two full speed-loaders as well as an extra full box of ammo. She'd shot with this gun many times and had begged him to bring it to school—just in case. But he'd always told her no.

It's been here all along?

She could just about squeal with excitement, but she kept it to herself. Since the power had gone out, and there was no background noises, she could hear conversations all the way down the hall, behind closed doors. That meant they could hear her too. And no doubt, she was probably the only kid in the college with a lethal weapon, and many would probably try to take it from her.

She climbed onto the bed and slid the pistol and ammo under her pillow. She picked up the letter again and continued reading.

. . .

know your first instinct is to want to come home the same way you would if you were driving. I don't know what the scenario is right now, but regardless, if there is an emergency, the interstate route isn't the way to come. It will be gridlocked. You could take Hwy. 29. It's back roads and rural. You'd still get here in nearly the same time, unless you're stuck in traffic. Bottom line, it's safer than the interstate and same drive-time.

If you're walking, don't take the highways or the interstate. It's not safe for you! Walking will take you much, much longer to get home than the normal one hour drive. You'll find a compass in this bag, with instructions. Read the instructions before you leave. If you don't understand how to use it, you may finally realize that daddy was right. Should have listened. But since you didn't, find yourself a nice boy scout to help you. You'll be following the compass through the woods. You'll have to cross roads and highways. Be alert! Hide until you know the coast is clear. Cross quickly and get back under cover. See the map. I marked that route for you.

I know you can do this, Graysie. I'm so proud of you, and I love you. Whenever you've set your mind to something in the past, it's been Katie, bar the door. So set your mind to this, and get your ass in gear.

Come home to me soon, baby girl.

Love,

Dad

Graysie's chin quivered as she held her hand over her mouth. Tears pricked at her eyes until finally, she left them flow. She rocked back and forth and squeezed her eyes shut.

She wanted her dad. This letter from him made it all too real. She was truly in deep shit. She couldn't do this alone. She didn't know how to read a compass. She dug in the bag and found the small army-green pouch. She opened it to find a folded instruction manual atop compass. Quickly, she scanned the instructions. It didn't make a lick of sense to her. She needed help.

The backpack was heavy. There was no way she could carry it all the way home, if she had to walk. Plus, she was sure her dad hadn't packed her any clothes. She'd need at least one spare set. She folded up the letter and put it back in the envelope, holding it up to her nose.

She couldn't smell him, but the memory of his clean scent still filled her nose.

Squeezing her eyes shut, she held the letter to her heart. Ivory soap and Old Spice. She teased him about the Old Spice, telling him it was for old men, but secretly she loved his old soul. He was forty years old this year. It seemed ancient to her, but a lot of her friends' dads were much older.

She dumped everything out on the bed, and then opened all the zippers and compartments, throwing everything into one big pile. Then she sorted into three groups: sanitation, survival and sustenance.

In the sanitation pile, she put a plastic baggie of too-little folded toilet paper—*too stingy on the tp, Dad*—and a small clear bag that she could see through. It contained a

toothbrush and toothpaste, Dove soap disposable wash-
cloths, and a small bottle of hand sanitizer. A tiny bottle
labeled bleach, and a ShamWow towel also went into that
pile. And lastly, a Diva Cup. *Ewww.* So maybe he wasn't as
squeamish about girl-stuff as she thought he was. She
giggled as she thought about him handling it. Although
still new in the box, he'd probably picked it up with
gloves on.

In the sustenance pile, she placed a compact Rocket
Stove. It was in a tiny orange case not much bigger than a
pack of smokes. The picture on the front showed someone
feeding pine cones and sticks into it. Super cool, since it
wasn't necessary to carry fuel. *Smart, Dad.*

She sorted a blue over-sized camp cup, a fork/spoon
combo attached to the top of a small mess kit, a water
bottle/filter combo, a canteen, water purification tablets,
and food: two vacuum-sucked pouches of what looked like
Stove Top Stuffing. Written on the side was a note: Add
boiling water. There was also beef jerky, two envelopes of
Instant Lipton Cup-a-Soup Chicken & Rice, a small jar of
peanut butter with honey, two energy bars and several
baggies of GORP—good 'ole fashioned raisins and peanuts
—and a can of tuna. The tuna had a note folded and taped
to the bottom. It said: "Tuna Torch: Can burn up to 3 hours
for light, and then be eaten. Unfold for instructions." A
tuna-scented candle? That ought to smell nice. *Not.*

She smirked and tossed it into the pile.

Into the survival pile she placed the folded map, an
emergency Life-Straw, a small first aid kit, a folded Mylar

blanket, a bundle of paracord, and a small mirror—Good. I can use that. Also, a pack of three Bic lighters, a small fishing kit in a tin Altoids box, an Army Swiss knife/multi-tool thingy, a poncho, bug deterrent wipes, water purification tablets, duct tape wrapped around a pencil, a bundle of wire, a hand-crank flashlight, and a bottle of Advil.

She was left with a cluster of zip ties—what the heck am I supposed to do with those? —a rolled-up hat with a brim, a stack of five surgical masks marked N95, several sets of latex gloves, goggles, a pile of small assorted clips, a bandana, and two brown medicine bottles.

She popped open the top of one of the medicine bottles to find cotton balls stuffed inside that smelled of petroleum jelly. She shoved the lid back and looked at the side of the bottle. In black sharpie her father had written in tiny letters: Use 1 to light fire. The other bottle held waterproof matches. She threw them into the survival pile.

She put aside the face masks and gloves. She wouldn't be needing those.

Digging deeper, to the very bottom, she found a large K-Bar U.S. Marine knife in a sheath and two pairs of good walking socks.

Graysie raised her eyebrows. It was a lot of stuff.

The hat looked slightly too big. She flipped it over to try it on and found another note taped to the inside.

"If you're walking, put up that hair! Try not to look like a girl. If someone messes with you, fight like a man."

She ripped the note off the hat, finding a hair-tie and some hair pins underneath.

She stuffed everything back in and grabbed a pair of jeans and two T-shirts. She twisted the clothes into tight rolls and crammed them in the top of the bag. Now to get some help figuring out this stupid compass.

She shoved the backpack under the bed and went in search of a boy scout.

GRAYSON TILTED his head up at the mountain of Puck. "Come on, son. What're you waiting for? Jump down here."

Puck stood balanced on the bumper of the truck, staring down at Ozzie, and rubbing his head with both hands. He mumbled incoherently and then shook his hands in the air. Tugging unnecessarily at his too-big pants, he flashed his ankles again as he stalled.

"What's the matter? I told ya, he won't bite."

Instead of jumping, Puck turned around and slowly climbed down, peeking over his shoulder at Ozzie in fear. When he stepped off into the gravel, Ozzie tucked his head and shoulders down with his butt wiggling up in the air and whined, asking for Puck's attention.

"Don't mind him. He's doing his doggie yoga," Grayson joked.

Puck giggled and hiked his pants up again. He bent down and hesitantly pet the dog, biting his lip in concentration. Soon, they were fast friends, with Puck throwing a stick and Ozzie fetching it while Puck chortled like a schoolboy with a very bad cold.

It was as though Grayson ceased to exist.

He left them to it and went in to get the burgers he had thawing on the counter. Regardless of his bizarre guest, it would be nice to not eat alone for the first time in days.

*P*uck stared down at his plate while Grayson tucked into his own food.

Oh, he's praying. Grayson felt bad for starting too soon. While he was a Christian—or at least he considered himself one; he did believe in God after all—he didn't often pray. Maybe he should. A small prayer for his family to finally show up safe and sound couldn't hurt.

He put his burger down and lowered his own head, and while waiting respectfully for Puck to finish, he tried to formulate some semblance of a prayer of his own. Giving up, he silently spoke to The Big Guy: *Just bring 'em home soon, God.*

A full minute passed and Grayson took a peek. Puck wasn't praying; he was staring at his food. A slow tear trailed down his cheek.

Awkward.

The kid was probably missing his mother. Grayson cleared his throat. "What's up, Puck?"

"I don't like lettuce. *Jenny* likes lettuce."

Oh for crying out loud.

Out of habit, Grayson had dressed Puck's burger the same way he did for his daughter, Graysie: loaded.

He sighed and stood up, pulled the top bun off the burger and snatched the lettuce off and then dropped the top back onto it and sat down. "There. No lettuce. Now eat."

Puck happily dug in as though the last few minutes hadn't happened. He sat with his legs spread wide, taking up nearly one entire side. He was a big man. *Or man-child.* He clumsily gobbled his first burger down in four bites, smearing ketchup and mustard around his mouth. The boy was starving. He swiped at his mouth with his arm and dug into the second burger on his plate.

"Use your napkin, Puck." Grayson lifted his own napkin and wiped his already-clean mouth in example. "How old are you?"

Puck frowned and rapid blinked his eyes. "Um... ten and eight?" he said through a mouth full of food.

"You're eighteen?"

Puck nodded and kept chewing.

"What have you been eating for the past few days while your mama's been gone?"

"Pork 'n beans, mostly. Mama Dee didn't get the circle lids last month. I can't open the others. If I bring them over here, can you open them for me, mister gray man?"

"Gray*son*. My name is Grayson. You don't have to call me mister, either. What's a circle lid?"

"The ones you pull the circle and the top comes off."

"Oh, a pull-top. I guess you can't open the others

because the power's off? Don't you have a handheld can opener?"

"Mama Dee does. I don't know how to work it. I'm the only one who can open the jars though. She said we could eat three jars while she was gone. I ate those the first day. And Jenny ate some, too."

"What was in the jars?"

"Mama Dee's veggie soup, and some slimy green leafy stuff—Jenny ate that—and apple sauce. Me and Jenny shared that one."

So Mama Dee knew how to can food. The green stuff sounded like collard greens. Or spinach. Hopefully she had a full pantry to feed Puck and Jenny until she returned.

"I think until Mama Dee gets back it would be okay to eat whatever you need, Puck. Just don't eat too much. Maybe stick to the canned food for now. I can show you how to open a can. Jenny doesn't know how either?"

"No."

Maybe Jenny was *special* too?

"So, you said Jenny's not your sister?"

"No. We're not really kin." Puck saved the last bite of his burger for Ozzie, who gently took it from his fingers and then closed his eyes as Puck rubbed his head and ran his hand down his back. The kid was obsessed with the dog. He'd seen Grayson pass Ozzie his own burger that was swallowed in pretty much one bite, but still shared his own food with him. Now that he was over his fear, he couldn't keep his hands off of the dog, petting him constantly. "But I *love* Jenny."

Grayson raised his eyebrows. *Love* like a sister? Or more? Maybe that's why she was sleeping in the barn instead of the house. "You mean you love her like you love Mama Dee?"

He shook his head. "No. *More*. Jenny is pretty. I like her hair." Puck smiled innocently.

Grayson studied the boy. With his size, maybe Jenny was sleeping in the barn because she was afraid of him. Maybe she didn't *love* Puck like Puck *loved* her...

"Listen, kid. While Mama Dee is gone, it might be best if you sleep in the barn and let Jenny sleep in the house. You're the man there, right? It makes more sense for the men to sleep outside."

Puck pursed his lips together. "I don't know if Mama Dee would like that. She doesn't let me sleep in the barn. I wish Jenny could just stay in the house with me. I'm scared."

Could be Mama Dee was more worried about the boy than the girl. He wasn't the sharpest tool in the shed and maybe he couldn't be trusted to fend for himself outside. And if he was so scared in the house, he'd probably be terrified in the barn at night. It really wasn't safe for either of them to be in the barn right now anyway, with those thugs having chased Puck up a tree. They might come back.

He'd never seen Puck's home, but the neighbors had described it as a dilapidated shack in a clearing in the woods; run-down and crumbling. He probably needed to go over and check on these kids himself. But would Mama Dee be okay with that? People who live in squalor usually didn't take kindly to strangers dropping by and maybe passing judgement.

"How many bedrooms is in your house, Puck?"

Puck held up first one finger, turned it around to look at it, and then another.

"Two? I'll tell you what. You tell Jenny about those bad kids. Tell her until Mama Dee comes back you *both* need to stay in the house. There's safety in numbers."

"But if Mama Dee gets mad, can I tell her you said so?"

"Absolutely. Tell her I said so. But listen, you two need to sleep in separate rooms, okay? Maybe Jenny can sleep in Mama Dee's bed." He gave Puck a very serious fatherly stare. "No kissing or anything like that, is what I mean."

Puck laughed—a loud honking noise that surprised both Grayson and Ozzie. "Jenny wouldn't like that, Gray Man." His angelic face turned solemn and wistful. With big eyes, he said, "Jenny lets me touch her hair sometimes. But then sometimes she gets mad and tries to kick me."

This was sounding more and more creepy. Grayson was concerned about these two kids being alone, but apparently Jenny knew how to handle Puck if he got too handsy. He seemed almost afraid of her.

He'd give it another day or so and if the power didn't come back on, he'd insist one or the other—or both—stay here until their mother returned.

If only he'd known how the woman of the house really felt about Jenny, and the danger she was in when Mama did return, he would have gone over and brought her home *that day.*

"IF I HAVE to watch you scratch your balls *one* more time..." Gabby threatened. It was sickening. The man—Larry—was sticking his hand directly down the front of his pants as though Gabby—or her sisters—weren't in the car with him.

Disgusting pig.

He laughed and continued to scratch as they hit a congested spot, all leaned back with one hand slung over the steering wheel. They crept down the highway meandering around the cars and crowds of people, and feeling as though they were being suffocated by the waves of heat coming up off the road. More than a dozen people had tried to stop their car, stepping out to the point of almost getting hit.

So many people were desperate, and she felt almost guilty that her circumstances were better. Not guilty enough to get out and walk with them, but it hurt her heart to see this. And it terrified her. If they hadn't run into Larry —regardless of what a jerk he was—they'd be walking too.

Gabby swallowed hard. It was making her sick. All of it. *He* was making her sick. Rude. Crude. No manners. Sweaty —and refusing to run the air because it might use too much gas—they were going stir crazy with him in the car. She could barely stand to look at him with his cul-de-sac of greasy hair fringing his shiny bald spot, cheap false teeth and sparkly gold chain.

He'd come on to each one of them in turn, especially Emma. He'd asked her to sit in the front before even starting the car. Gabby made sure she stepped up instead. She could handle assholes like this much better than Emma and Olivia; they were too nice.

She dug into her bag and came out with a container of Monkey Butt. It was powder that was used for chafing. She and her sisters—and their husbands—had used it for years, especially in the summer when they'd be exercising and sweating. She tossed it at Larry, who missed the catch, letting it roll down between his legs into the floor.

She grimaced. "You need to use that."

"Get it." He raised an eyebrow and smirked at her.

She rolled her eyes and looked away.

They'd been on the road with him an excruciating two hours and had just barely made fifty miles. The back roads had been nearly completely blocked with broken-down cars out of gas. Getting around the stalled congestion from behind a bottleneck of other still-mobile cars had been like trying to thread a needle, especially with Larry driving and treating his sacred car as though it were made of glass. He'd finally detoured and hit the interstate instead and they'd made a bit of progress, although the situation was much the same. Miles of interstate was gridlocked. They were able to barely eat up miles by alternating between driving on the shoulder and weaving between stalled vehicles on the highway.

Hordes of people were walking in groups and many were alone along the highway. They walked on the road more times than not. Several had jumped out of his way just in time to avoid a bloody collision and Larry had hit the horn so much that Gabby was suffering with a near-blinding headache. At this point, it would probably be faster to walk, if only Olivia had some walking shoes.

A sign for a rest area came up and Gabby pointed it out, hoping Larry would take her up on her offer of sharing her Monkey Butt, and she and the girls could also find somewhere to relieve themselves. Assuming they'd be home soon, they'd all drank a bottle of water to re-hydrate. Gabby was also hoping for a hand-pump to fill their bottles up with before getting back on the road; she'd seen them at rest areas before.

Larry swerved into the parking lot amidst another wave of people.

The situation was even worse here.

The ladies looked around as Larry slowly drove through.

"This is creepy," Emma said. "Looks like the walking dead."

"Yeah, let's just keep going," Gabby answered.

Larry shrugged. "We're here now. We won't stay long."

Refugees who had probably been on their way to or from the beach, just trying to eke out enough miles to get to the next exit for available gas were camped out in cars, tents, or tarps thrown over tree branches. Clothes hung from branches and trash littered the grounds. Hundreds of people were laying in the tents, under the tarps or just on the grass. Small campfires dotted the landscape. At a glance, anyone could see the people were tired, hungry, thirsty and downright dirty.

Gabby could feel desperation in the air. This wasn't a happy crowd at all, but for the most part they looked like a harmless band of gypsies.

So far.

And there wasn't a hand-pump for water in sight.

They slid into a parking spot beside an SUV that was obviously being used as housing. The back door was up for airflow, and blankets and pillows were haphazardly arranged inside. Two small children lay curled around each other in the back, asleep. Their mother and father were kicked back in the front seats, their legs tangled together on the dash, with all the windows down.

Larry climbed out the car, stretching and rubbing behind him, trying to bring blood back to his flat ass. He caught Gabby staring at him. "How's it look?" He waggled an eyebrow at her.

She gave him a look of disgust. "Flat as a fritter from where I'm standing."

He laughed it off and grabbed the talc from the floor. "Y'all stay with the car. I'll be right back," he said, adjusting his junk before he swaggered off.

"Take your time, not mine," Gabby mumbled, marveling at his rudeness. What ever happened to ladies first?

She gazed around the make-shift campsites, suddenly noticing several men standing up, giving them the dirty eyeball. Two out of the largest group slowly made their way toward them.

"Emma, reach into my bag and get the gun," she whispered. "If anyone tries to take the car, we need to be ready."

Olivia was still sitting in the back seat looking at their highlighted route on the map that was paper-clipped to a picture of her and Gabby standing arm in arm in front of Jake's truck, Ruby. She looked up in alarm. "Who's going to try to take the car?" she asked loudly.

"*Shhh!*" Gabby flashed wide eyes at her and jerked her head toward the men.

Emma dug through and pulled out the gun, stepped up beside Gabby and discreetly slid it to her. "Here, you take it."

Gabby pushed it into the waistband at the back of her pants and stared back at the men defiantly. "If they try to take it, you both know what to do."

"Fight like a man," Emma whispered.

Olivia stepped up beside her sisters, more out of curiosity than bravery.

The men approached to within hearing distance when Gabby yelled, "Stop right there."

"Gabby! Don't be rude," Olivia admonished her. "Maybe they just want to talk."

"Shut up, Olivia. This is not the time for strangers to just want to talk. We've got a working car. They don't," she answered.

All three of the men looked mean, exhausted and angry.

One spoke up, "How much gas do you have?"

Gabby slid over far enough to hopefully block their view from the five-gallon jug sitting in the middle of the back seat. The rest were in the trunk. "Not much. Enough for a few more miles, probably, before we're walking," she lied. "How about you all? Is everyone stuck here?"

"Yeah, no. We just like living in a rest area," he answered sarcastically and then sighed and rubbed his hands over his face in desperation. "Look, we got kids. Lots of them, and they're in no shape to walk."

There were dozens of kids, and they did look lethargic and weak. Kids didn't normally lay down in the middle of the day on road trips. They ran, played, and laughed. Life was usually one big game to them, regardless of the situation. But everywhere they could see, these kids were huddled up on dirty blankets and pillows, or laying with their heads in their mother's laps on the ground, or in cars.

They couldn't help them all. They might be able to squeeze one or two in between them, but they'd need a bus to move this many children. Gabby nodded. "I understand.

But like I said, we've only got enough to get a little farther down the road, and then we'll be parked and stuck too, and we'll be walking. I'm sorry we can't help you."

"Got any water?"

"No."

"Any food?"

Gabby looked at Emma. She nodded and reached into the car, pulling out Gabby's backpack. She dug through it, pulling out random food stuff.

The men hurried forward.

"No! Stop where you are. We'll throw it over to you," Gabby insisted, pulling out the gun and letting it hang beside her in full view, ready to aim.

Not surprisingly, they listened.

As Gabby kept a close eye on the men, Emma and Olivia threw the food; a bag of gorp, a can of spam, and a few energy bars. They gave them everything they could quickly find.

Larry wandered up just as they finished passing the food over. "What's going on?"

Gabby stepped in close to speak to him, cringing at his breath. "These guys were asking about the car and gas. We can't help them, but we gave them some food."

"Yeah. Hell no, I can't help 'em. Let's go," he whispered, his eyes darting all over in fear.

"Uh... what about us, Larry? We need to use the... we need to pee," Gabby whispered.

Olivia stepped up to whisper too, "I can't wait another mile. Look at that end over there. Let's drive that way as though we're leaving and get away from this crowd, but then we can pull over and hurry into the woods and back. It'll only take a few minutes."

On the exit ramp leaving the rest area, there were only a few vehicles, looking long-abandoned, and only two women were in that area, far away from the group. They were laying down under a tree and appeared to be asleep. It was a good plan.

Or good enough.

Larry sighed as though it was a huge inconvenience, ignoring the fact he'd also needed and had taken a pit stop. "Alright, but you girls better hurry," he grumbled.

They piled back into the car and slowly drove to the other end, almost to the on-ramp to re-enter the interstate. Larry pulled over and the girls jumped out. Gabby grabbed her bag and seeing her map and picture had slid to the floor, she snatched those up too and slid them into her back pocket.

"Why are you taking all that just to go pee?" he asked.

"Toilet paper," she snapped at him, and then turned to run behind her sisters to the nearby stand of trees. The truth was, she didn't trust him.

The two women lying near the trees weren't asleep after all. Clothes torn and dirty, and hair in knots, they were in terrible shape. They wore low-cut shirts and too-tight shorts with strappy, high heels. They both gripped their arms just below an angry-red mark on their shoulders, like a fresh burn, in the shape of the number "2."

The women were clearly prostitutes, yet they cast narrowed and judging eyes upon Gabby and her sisters.

One of the ladies shook her head in disgust as they ran by, and Gabby wondered what that was all about, but it was too late. Her bladder had anticipated relief and she was on a countdown at the moment. She hurried to catch up with Olivia and Emma.

If only they'd heard the words thrown at them as they ran by, they might have stopped and avoided the disaster about to come their way.

"Ass, grass, or gas..." the woman called after them.

J A K E   S K I D to a stop at the closed gate to QualPro Auto & Marine, a local repair shop that shared property with a used car and marine dealership—both owned by the same guy. He jumped off the 4-wheeler, and made his way around the closed gate to the door. The shop was less than five miles from his house, and if he was going to be stuck out a Grayson's for any period of time, he'd need something to do to keep busy, and he needed his own truck anyway. One more part and Ruby would be ready to roll.

He scanned the parking lot as he walked. *What the heck?* He took it all in as he reached for the door handle.

"Stop right there," a female voice barked out.

Jake stopped abruptly and whipped around, looking for the voice.

Most of the cars from the front lines had been pulled into the middle of the lot into a haphazard cluster, barely seen behind the wall of boats that surrounded them. On top of an old Pontoon boat was a woman, laying prone on the sun deck behind a deer rifle mounted on a tripod, hair tucked beneath a camo-colored ball cap. Even from this distance, Jake could see one big blue eye opposite the other eye hovering behind the scope. He caught a glimpse of her jet-black pony-tail riding behind the cap.

It was Rena, Nick's girlfriend and office manager.

"We're closed! What do you need?"

"Where's Nick?" Jake asked.

"Right here," a deep voice boomed from a few boats over.

A hand waved from the cabin window in the belly of a cuddy cabin, long enough for Jake to see it, and then pulled back in. "Like she said, we're closed, unless you're trading. You looking to swap in that 4-wheeler?"

Jake squinted at the face in the window, seeing nothing but the short salt & pepper-colored beard and dark sunglasses, but it was definitely Nick. He shook his head. "Naw, man. I'm just here to pick up the part for my truck."

"Unless you got something other than money to trade for it, I ain't open for business. I'll take food, ammo, gas or guns. Or the 4-wheeler, like I said."

"Trade? I already paid for the part. It's me...Jake. That part is for my '57 Chevy. You said it'd be here a week ago. I just got around to getting here."

There was a long pause during which Jake spotted one of Nick's mechanics, sitting portside of another boat, still as a statue, with a long-gun pointed Jake's way. A rustle of fabric drew his eye to yet another mechanic, who up until now had been quiet as a mouse standing in the back of a 4x4 truck, gun resting on the top of the cab—again, pointed at Jake.

Jake slowly raised his hands against the four guns pointing at him. "What's going on here, Nick? Why you got all your cars and boats jammed in together like that? And what's with the sniper patrol? You see some trouble already?"

Jake spoke to the boat he'd glimpsed Nick in, but the window was empty. A few thumps later and Nick jumped out onto the concrete, swinging his rifle to let it hang from the strap behind his shoulder. "Yeah dude, I'm sorry. I forgot all about you already having paid for that part. I got it for you. All hell has been breaking loose. This is the first break I've had from looky-loos, criminals and assholes trying to get a' hold of one of my cars for nothing. Everybody needs gas and they're hoping my cars and boats are all filled up. Their cars are broke down all over town."

"They all running?" Jake asked.

"Hell yeah, they ran. Not many men will stand still with a woman pointing a rifle at 'em!"

Jake laughed. "No, I meant the cars. They're all gassed up?"

Nick shrugged. "They're not all full, if that's what you're asking. If a person was to siphon all the gas, they'd probably get more than a few tanks out of it. But everybody

seems to think I'm giving my shit away for free," he grumbled as he approached the door, jumbling his keys around
to find the right one. "They'd just as soon take one and
drive it as far as it'll go."

He led Jake into the shop and walked behind the
counter. Jake stepped up as he had dozens of times and
there was his part, sitting right on top with '1957 Chevy
Truck' scribbled on the box; Nick was his go-to person for
parts for just about anything, as well as who Jake himself
used for car repairs and oil changes for Gabby's car. He'd
stopped doing it himself years ago when he and Gabby
started making enough money to send it to the shop. The
little bit of free time he got away from his own work as a
mechanic, or time with Gabby, was better spent tinkering
with Ruby or helping the family out on the farm. Both
Grayson and Dusty brought their stuff to Nick too. Nick was
pretty much the only mechanic the entire family trusted.
He was downright cantankerous at times, but he was
honest.

Just a few months ago, Grayson had mentioned Nick
had finally sewed up a long battle of a divorce, which was
the cause of most of his cantanker-isms. Twenty years with
the she-devil had buried Nick under layers of stress and
debt. Whoever had said it was cheaper to keep 'er obviously
hadn't met Nick's wife. As Nick ran his finger over the
paperwork rack on the wall, Jake took stock of him. He'd
lost a lot of weight. The divorce had dragged on for several
years, leaving Nick wiry, weary and whiskery.

And then once that was buttoned up, he'd jumped right out of the fire and into the frying pan with Rena. At least five years younger and could be a howling hellcat, but at least this one had a heart of gold, ran the office like a well-oiled machine, and could also hunt, fish and turn a wrench, if she wanted or needed to. They were a good match.

The fact that Nick owned the place but more times than not wore a uniform and crawled up in and under things with or without his team earned him respect, with both his staff and his customers. He was a hell of a mechanic. Best in the state, the rumor was.

Jake's eyes widened when he looked behind the counter. Four cardboard boxes crowded the space behind the register, stuffed with mostly canned goods; metal cans as well as glass jars of homemade preserved food. Colorful pickled vegetables, collard greens and jam and jellies caught his eye. Behind that row of boxes sat two more heaped high with miscellaneous things. Toilet paper, cigarettes and even a few bottles of liquor topped the heap.

Seven five-gallon gas jugs stood sentry over the food as the final row.

"What's all that for? You living here?" Jake nodded at the stuff.

"Trading here. At least until the last of the gas is gone. Two of us will be taking this stuff over to the house later," Nick answered as he slid the part to Jake with a paper slip and pen for signing the receipt. Jake almost chuckled that he was still following office procedure when he and his staff were all outside, armed to the huckleberries, circling the wagons. Probably worried that Rena would have his hide if he skipped a step. Nick was the boss, but Rena ran a tight ship behind that counter.

Jake scribbled his name and slid the paper back to Nick. "You've been busy if you got all that in two days. So you're not taking money at all?"

"I could have bought all that and more with the sale of one used car before the lights went out, and I wish like hell right now I would've. But no. I'm not taking cash. Ain't nothing to buy with it. Stores are already bare bones. What good is it?"

Jake shrugged. "It looks like you're all set for a while anyway."

Nick shook his head. "Nope. That won't last long. I didn't have much at the house when the lights went out. Grocery store was wiped out the first day the power was gone. Gas stations aren't pumping anymore. I got plenty of money and nowhere to spend it. I wish I'd listened to your brother-in-law when he'd talk about all that being prepared shit. I did get lucky. I got something people need right now. But hell, what I've gotten in return so far won't last us a month. Rena and I are feeding my boy, too." He shrugged his shoulders. "We need numbers, though. Can't get no damn sleep if there's only two of you, even if Rena is a hell of a shot."

"You already had trouble out at the house, too?" Jake asked, concerned. Nick lived ten miles from him, but closer to town.

"Hell yeah we have. Bunch of damn rednecks came looking for food last night. They left rather quick-like, especially considering they probably had a bit of buckshot in their asses for their trouble. But they'll be back, or more of 'em. It ain't safe nowhere near town."

Jake nodded. He wouldn't head back to the house. It would just be a waste of gas. If trouble had already found Nick's neighborhood, it wouldn't be long until it found his. He trusted Tucker would be on top of it. He was heading straight to Grayson's place. He'd just have to get the 4-wheeler back later.

As though Nick read his mind, he said, "Say, how's Grayson doing out at his place? I know he's prepared. And he's far enough out there it'll take a while before he sees company. But when he does," Nick shook his head again. "He got numbers to watch his six?"

Jake wasn't positive, but felt pretty sure it was just Grayson there right now. However, it wasn't his place to invite anyone, nor did he want anyone to know they might not have enough protection, even if it was Nick, whom they all knew and liked.

"Yeah. He's got a house full. Bunch of buddies, plus Dusty. You know Dusty is a cop, right? He brought some of his crew with him, too."

Nick sighed and Jake felt bad for the lie.

"Look, if there's room for y'all, we'll find a way to get back to you and tell you. Maybe you can load up what you got and come out there. But don't come unless one of us comes to get you. Might not be room enough for y'all and those cops are trigger nervous. That work?"

Nick looked relieved at the possibility. "Yeah. You tell Grayson we'll pull our weight and then some. We'll be ready to go once all this gas is gone." He waved at the gas tanks lined up behind him. "And I don't think that'll take more than a day or so."

"I'll tell him." Jake gave him a nod and turned to go.

"Hey, Jake," Nick said, "What color is your Chevy?"

"Red. Ruby red. Why?"

Nick shook his head. "I thought so. We had a group of bikers in here yesterday looking for bike parts. One of them saw this box and asked about it and asked where you live. He was looking for a red one. I know you work on it out at Grayson's but I told him I didn't know where you lived."

"You tell him the color?"

Nick scoffed. "Yeah, I did. But I told him it was *yellow*. I'm not stupid."

"Thanks, man. Why was he asking?"

"State-wide Biker-Scavenger hunt. Those things are big deals for bikers and it was on their list. You should have seen that convoy. Beat all I ever saw. One biker had a pig—a live pig in a purple skirt—strapped to the back of his bike."

"No shit?"

"Yeah, apparently a red '57 Chevy was on the list too. But they moved on, headed south toward the beach."

Jake's blood ran cold. "You know which beach?"

Nick shook his head. "I wasn't asking any questions. That crew wasn't too friendly. I gave them all the bike parts

I had on the house and sent them on their way. I was just glad I didn't have all this food and stuff sitting out here when they came through. They're part of the baddest biker gang in the Carolinas. Looking for trouble. You be careful out there, you hear?"

"Will do," Jake answered. "And you might want to stack that stuff in the back until you get it hauled out of here."

Nick stepped forward and shook his hand. He glanced around, giving the area outside the gate where Jake was parked a once-over, nodded a final goodbye and turned to head back into the shop.

Jake looked around him for any signs of trouble. All was quiet next door at the shopping strip mall and drugstore. But for the first time he noticed the windows of all those businesses had been broken out and the drugstore was now boarded up and closed for business.

His heart fell. That was his next stop, and the most important.

Loose items littered the parking lot; clothes, empty boxes, bits and pieces of something or the other. They were probably cleaned out before they were boarded up. Other than the part for Ruby, this was a wasted run and wasted gas.

On the other side of the shopping strip was a run-down residential property that was well-known to be frequented by drunks and rednecks squatting there for days on end. Piles of beer cans littered the yard most Mondays when he passed by on his way to work.

Lots of activity over there. It was a small crowd of probably ten or fifteen people and Jake could hear them yelling, although he couldn't make out the words. Probably just drunk and rowdy.

He shoved the part for Ruby into the saddle-bag on the back and climbed onto the 4-wheeler feeling nervous about the ride to Grayson's. He fired up the engine, getting the attention of the crowd.

"Hey!" someone yelled. Two men broke away from the group and walked toward him. Jake squinted, trying to determine if he knew the men. It'd be nice to talk to someone. Trade information at the very least, maybe find out what anyone was saying about the power being out.

Jake threw his hand up in a friendly wave. "Hey."

One of the men shoved the other, viciously pushing him to the ground and broke into a brisk run. "I saw it first!" he yelled.

The 4-wheeler. They want it.

A handful of others split from the crowd and ran toward Jake, mere seconds behind the first two. Soon, they'd all be on him.

He quickly put the ATV in reverse.

The engine died.

He tried to start it again.

It turned over, over, and over...but didn't fire.

Oh shit. Jake had no idea how old the battery was. *Hell, where's a mechanic when you need one*, he thought in panic, looking up to see if Nick had heard the problem and come back out—hopefully carrying his gun.

No sign of Nick.

One more time, he tried it, chanting 'please' under his breath and hoping he wasn't flooding it with too much gas. He looked over his shoulder. Two of the men had put some distance in front of the others. They were close. He studied their desperate faces for a second. He didn't know either of them and they certainly weren't running to help.

Jake's heart raced.

He could hear his blood rushing through his ears.

Panic settled over him in a cold sweat. He couldn't hold off a crowd of five men alone.

He looked for Nick; he wasn't there.

Then, another glance over his shoulder.

Two of the men were fifty feet away and gaining fast. They looked like a couple of thugs.

Could this get violent? Over a 4-wheeler? Had life gone from normal to this in two days?

Finally, the engine turned over. He shifted into reverse and whipped the 4-wheeler around, nearly running over the first of the men to reach him.

Suddenly, Jake was whipped off the ATV with an elbow around his neck and thrown to the ground. He hit the pavement hard enough to rattle his teeth, landing on his ass. Tucker would kill him if his 4-wheeler was stolen. He came off the ground in a crouch spewing a burst of obscenities and lunging forward in a rush of adrenaline.

His attacker threw a leg over and landed precariously, barely on the seat, but frantically turned the handlebars to make his getaway.

Before Jake could take the four steps back to the ATV,

his attacker was thrown off and landed at Jake's feet. The second thug was on the bike now.

Jake and his attacker both leapt in tandem to reach the second man who was seconds away from gone, knocking him off the bike in a jumble of fists.

A sharp elbow cracked Jake in the forehead, knocking him back down and stunning him a second. He shook it off and sprung to his feet, and pitched forward to catch the 4-wheeler by the back rack; it was rolling away.

His hand was nearly jerked off the bike as another attack had him on his back foot, being pulled from behind. He tried to hold his ground but the ferocity of the assault was intense; he fought to pull forward but it wasn't long before he took one step back, then another. He let go, made a sudden turn and swung behind him. The heel of his hand caught the man on the chin with the force of his body behind the blow. Jake heard something snap and the hoodlum hit the ground, only replaced by the other attacker, who took Jake down with one sweep of his foot and hopped on the bike like a cowboy at a rodeo, hooting his success.

Jake cursed his bad leg and reached behind him, pulling out the pistol he had tucked into the back of his pants, drawing it as he fell, thinking *this can't be happening.* He hadn't been in a fist fight since eighth grade, and he remembered why; it hurt like hell. He couldn't think straight; fear and confusion clouded his mind.

What was he doing pulling a gun?

How had things ratcheted up to this level?

His finger found the trigger as his body smacked the pavement, jarring his spine.

A loud boom cracked through the air and Jake watched the thug fall from the bike in slow motion, hit the ground and lay still, while the other hooligan froze and then ran the opposite way.

"YOU TWO GO FIRST," Gabby offered.

Olivia and Emma squatted while Gabby watched out for them, hopping from one foot to the other and constantly looking from the large group of people on one end of the rest area to Larry on the other end, hoping he wouldn't leave them.

They were stupid. One of them should've stayed with Larry and the car. It wasn't like he had any morals or ethics, at least as far as she could see. Gabby didn't doubt for one second he'd leave them, if he could part Olivia from her watch first, and he still had their T-shirt bags full of stuff.

Emma jumped and pulled her pants up. "Did you hear that?"

"What?" Gabby asked. She and Olivia cocked their heads, listening.

Olivia stood and jerked her pants up too, nodding with wide eyes. "I hear it."

Farther into the woods, behind them, a small sound carried on the wind.

Gabby couldn't wait any longer. She squatted. "Just a minute. I can't wait. One of you watch that way and the other watch the rest area. Make sure those guys stay on their side and Larry doesn't leave us."

She hurried to take care of her business and then stood too, ready to go. "Come on."

"No, Gabby. Listen. It sounds like a kitten," Olivia whispered. "Or a baby..."

They stood very still. There it was again, but this time over the wood-bugs and birds chirping and chipping, they also heard a grunting noise. "Sounds like a wild pig," Emma whispered. "*And* a kitten."

Gabby grabbed Emma and Olivia's arms and squeezed. "Wild pigs will attack you. They have tusks. They're *very* dangerous," she whispered. "Let's go back to the car."

"No. We have to go look," Olivia whispered. She pushed the branches apart and stepped further into the woods, with Emma following closely behind.

Gabby threw her hands up into the air. "If it's a pig, you better be able to climb a tree fast or back up and sneak away. Seriously, it can kill you..."

Emma and Olivia weren't listening to her. They were too intent on their crusade to worry about their own fates. "Sure, I'll stay here and keep an eye on Larry," Gabby whispered sarcastically to herself.

*W*hen the brush thinned, Olivia and Emma stepped through a near wall of Live Oaks and straight into a scene torn from a horror movie.

Or Mad Max.

Olivia gasped and Emma threw out an arm, trying to stop her sister from walking too far in and getting discovered. But it was too late; no going back.

Strapped to the back of a motorcycle, furiously wiggling to trying to free itself from the tight straps, was a small white pig, barely more than a piglet. It gave one last weak grunt and then dropped its head in exhaustion, now laying limp across the leather seat.

It was wearing a purple ruffled tutu.

But on the ground, in a far worse position, a young Asian woman lay on her stomach hugging the earth, with one biker hovering over the top of her. His pants were pulled down below his knees. Two other rough-looking men stood next to them, watching. Or waiting their turn?

The man froze for a moment, but then with a grin at Olivia and Emma, he continued his rutting into the woman, whose body trembled, but otherwise stayed still. The fight was out of her. She was outnumbered and outmuscled— and she was handicapped.

One arm ended in a delicate stump at the wrist. It wasn't a new injury, not like the burning, curling skin on the shoulder of that same arm. The woman lay very still as though waiting for it to be over. She stared at Emma and

Olivia with startling almond-shaped blue eyes that
contrasted against her shiny, straight, long black hair. She
whimpered; a small sound as though a mewling kitten was
huddled within her ripped-open shirt. Her small breasts
were bared, her short skirt pulled up.

Time seemed to almost stop.

Almost.

In slow motion, as Emma and Olivia stood in open-
mouthed shock, he thrust once more with a groan and then
stood and tugged his faded jeans up and buckled a heavy
black belt, not bothering to hide his manhood as he did. He
smiled at Olivia and Emma.

The man had no shame. He jerked on the bottom edges
of his patch-filled leather vest covering his rippled, tattooed
chest as though to straighten it and gave a proud nod with
his chin.

His crew laughed in approval.

A long-handled branding iron lay against a tree, still
pink with heat, like the bubbled and ripped flesh on the
woman's arm. She'd been branded with an oversized
number "2".

Olivia sniffed. The smell of recently burnt human skin
wafted in the air. It preceded a buzzing that filled Olivia's
head; a sound so strong it blocked out the image in front of
her. She found herself not in the woods with a trio of bikers
and the woman on the ground, but back in the basement of
a house, where she herself had nearly been raped a few
years ago. Grayson had tried to find her to save her but he

was almost too late—she'd had to save herself. She shook off a shiver and tamped down the terrifying memory.

In a quiet voice, she mumbled, "Fight," the same word she'd heard in her own head in her dead mother's voice that night.

The girl looked straight at her, seeing her word. It seemed no one else was making a sound; or somehow, she and Olivia had forged a connection. "How? They're men," she mumbled back.

Or did she?

"Fight like a *man*," Olivia answered. Words she'd heard her husband say to his daughter.

But the woman had no fight left in her.

"Get up," Olivia screamed.

The biker looked at his crew and shrugged with a smile. "Next!"

The Asian woman didn't move. Resigned to her fate, she didn't cover herself either.

Emma grabbed Olivia's arm. "Let's go, Olivia."

Olivia jerked her arm away. "If another one of you touch her, I'll kill you."

The other two bikers stopped in their tracks, and then laughed out loud. Neither Olivia nor Emma held a weapon, nor were they a match for even one of the bikers, no less three.

The biker who had just finished with the woman—the obvious leader of the group—stepped forward. He was a giant of a man with a short gray high-and-tight haircut that looked more fitting for a military man than a biker. Engraved on his vest was his name: "Trunk," and on his bicep, was the word "TWO."

He bowed and mockingly waved an enormous arm pulsing with bulging veins and covered in ink toward the little clearing where the woman still lay. "Welcome *ladies*. You can join the party. It's not how it looks. She agreed to it," he nodded toward the Asian woman, "or you can get the hell out."

"Yeah, looks like she's really into it," Olivia muttered.

Emma shushed her and squeezed her arm. They both shook with fear, trembling against each other, shoulder to shoulder. "Then we can leave... with her?" Emma asked in a quiet voice.

Trunk smirked. "*You* ladies can leave, but not her. You can even take the other two sniveling bitches waiting out in the rest area. Don't need 'em. Done had 'em."

He looked back to the woman on the ground. "But this one's my new Old Lady. An Asian with *blue* eyes and a missing paw—believe it or not, that's *on the list*—she's worth three-hundred points on the scavenger hunt," he finished, looking at his buddies and winking. "As you can see, we take our scavenger hunts very seriously." He pointed to the pig and laughed. "She's definitely riding out of here with me and the pig."

"You can't just *take* someone," Emma snapped in false bravado.

The smile slid off Trunk's face. "Nobody's *taking* anything here. This bitch is giving it away—for food and water. Just like the other two who just left here," he spit out between gritted teeth. "She ain't no princess. She was a lot lizard before the grid went down. This is a *promotion*."

He and his buddies loudly laughed and bumped fists.

Olivia squatted down so she could be level to the Asian woman. "We've got food and water where we're going." The woman's eyes filled with tears. "Get up and come with us," Olivia pleaded. The woman continued to lay still at Trunk's feet, not willing to provoke him.

Emma tried to negotiate. "What would you trade for her?"

Trunk's voice roared, "I said no. She *stays*. Now get the fuck out of here before you two are staying with her." He snarled at them, knotting his fists into two huge balls, scaring them both to their core as he stood his ground over the woman.

Olivia gazed around at the three men and their campsite. Other than three nearly naked motorcycles—none of them sporting saddlebags—they had very little gear. A small campfire held a pot. Several empty beer bottles and food cans lay discarded beside a clear sack filled with water bottles. As far as she could see, they didn't have weapons either. The other two bikers look amused and not prepared for anything other than complete obedience to their leader.

She looked again at the woman on the ground and thought she saw a tiny glimmer of hope in her eyes as she stared back at Olivia, so she stood and took a deep breath and squeezed Emma's hand, and whispered almost silently, hoping Emma could hear her, "Fight like a man, little sister."

She turned and put her hands up to cup her mouth. She screamed at the top of her lungs, "*Gabby!* It's a pig! Come shoot it! Hurry!"

18

JAKE

JAKE LOOKED up in shock at Nick who had appeared out of thin air, standing tall and ready with his rifle pointed at the man on the ground. The other two mechanics ran up and slid to a stop, staring with wide eyes at the mayhem that had landed at their gate.

"Hurry up and get out of here," Nick yelled at Jake. "We got ya covered."

Jake lay on his back propped up with one elbow. He stared at his other hand which held a gun; a gun he couldn't even remember pulling out. Snapshots of his life with Gabby flashed through his mind. He'd screwed it up. In one moment, he'd killed their life together. Nothing would ever be the same again. Gabby would be devastated.

"I shot him," he mumbled.

His hand trembled and his nervous system took over, producing a wave of shakes that made it impossible for him to hold the gun. He carefully laid it down and looked up at Nick.

"I shot a man, Nick," he mumbled again through the fog in his head.

Nick shook his head. "No, you didn't. I did. Now get the hell outta here."

Jake looked around in confusion. "Are you sure?"

"Yeah, I'm sure. You didn't even shoot. If you don't believe me, I'll poke you in the ass with the spitting end of this rifle and you'll see how hot it is. That was *my* bullet." He nodded toward the man on the ground. The thug wasn't moving at all.

Blood puddled under him and ran into a crack on the pavement, making a dark river that ran toward where Jake lay. He scooted back in a hurry.

Surely, it didn't kill him?

As though Nick could read his thoughts, he said, "It's self-defense, Jake. Ain't no one coming up in my house beating people up and stealing shit. Now go before the rest of those guys make it over. I'll handle 'em."

Jake turned to look. Some of the other people had stopped in the middle of the parking lot, but two rough-looking men were heading their way. They'd be here in a minute at the most.

"The police might—"

"—dammit, Jake, there is no police. They weren't here when I was under attack and having to defend my gas, and they ain't coming now. You said you got cops at Grayson's place. Tell them your story if you need to. But not *here*. Not *now*. Go!" he yelled.

The ATV had rolled to a stop against the curb with the motor still running. Jake struggled to his feet and picked up the gun, turning it over in his hand.

Suddenly he remembered.

It wasn't loaded—and he had not a bullet one.

He jumped on the ATV and hauled ass home.

GRAYSIE THREW herself back onto her bed in frustration. She was on her own, and it was getting late. She was exhausted and home-sick. She *needed* to get home.

She'd gone looking for her boy scout, and came back empty-handed and disgusted. Out of the only three guys she would trust to take a road trip with—and that she could trust her dad not to kill upon first glance—two were drunk and the other was high. Their dorm was a tsunami of beer-pong with red Solo cups, empty food packages and weed bongs, all underneath an overwhelming smell of raw sewage.

In the shape she'd found them in, they couldn't find their way out of a wet paper bag. They'd be useless on the road, riding or walking, and even more useless with a compass. She couldn't believe *no one* was taking this seriously and making a plan.

Probably like Becky, they were expecting their mommy

or daddy or the *gooberment* to swoop in and fix this mess. Or they were assuming the power would be back on soon, even though communications were down too. She doubted any of them had *ever* watched the news, but especially in the last year, or the last *week*.

They had no idea Trixler was pissing off world leaders left and right and that this very well could be an attack on the United States. In Trixler's mission to make America great again, he was burning bridges faster than he was building them. But he *was* keeping his promises and making progress, even without those bridges.

Graysie disagreed with some of his policies, and she thought he was a disgusting male chauvinist pig and most likely a bit racist, but even she had to admit, he was *getting it done*.

And that confused her. She wasn't sure anymore who she was behind, or which side of the line her loyalties lay. She selfishly wanted America fixed for her future, but was Trixler really fixing it, or setting them up for war either amongst their own population or even their enemies abroad?

Was *this* war?

She and many of her friends and coeds had been behind Bernie; most of them not even sure just *why* they were behind Bernie, except that Bernie was cool in a nutty professor, or *Back To The Future* sort of way. They'd needed someone to get behind, and he'd fit the bill.

Especially after the bird.

During a Bernie rally it seemed as though he had called

the bird forth, right out of the sky. It sat on his podium, watched by thousands of people both in-person and online. Bernie said it was symbolism for a dove, asking for world peace. It was a lucky bit of political magic is what Graysie had thought of it at the time. He'd won many followers after that when the best the other candidates could do was unknowing spit a glob of food from their mouth, giving them the perfect target for a zillion memes and GIF's, or perform a little sarcastic and spooky shoulder-shimmy, or just throw childish insults about the size of hands and other body parts.

The election was all about entertainment for them... who could wow them or make them laugh the most...and Bernie's bird had really grabbed their attention.

It was sad.

When Bernie dropped out, half of her friends threw their support behind Hillary, and the other half stepped behind Trixler.

It didn't matter to her who was in office. It was just a face and a name. Her father's daughter, she was more worried about straightening out the economy and strengthening America, rather than personal opinions on race, color, gender, or sexual orientation.

After the election, her friends split again. Trixler haters versus Trixler supporters. Some just wanted a reason to protest. Some *wanted* to riot. They wanted a cause that would allow them to rally and scream and threaten and act like badly-behaved children. The other side pranced around in Trixler sweatshirts, flashing MAGA signs and trying to be cool when in reality they hadn't even voted. Both sides waited in anticipation for every Trixler tweet to broadcast so they could fight it out in the comments in an online twitter-war, one hundred and forty characters at a time.

It was ridiculous.

She watched it all from a distance, feeling older than her years. While they fussed between them every chance they got over what *wasn't* happening, she sat back and watched what *was* happening. She was shocked to see that in six months with Trixler in office, there were a million new jobs in the Unites States, the unemployment rate was at a ten-year low, and illegal immigration was down by huge numbers, which freed up even *more* jobs and benefits for Americans.

This stuff *mattered.*

Who was responsible for it didn't.

When and if they ever graduated college, they'd need a job.

Her friends *had* actually paid attention and cheered the imposed sanctions on Russia and North Korea. They agreed with Trixler for attempting to put America back into the big-brother position America rightly deserved by not letting bullies take advantage of us, or making us look bad, but what they didn't realize was that *also* put us more at risk for pissing them off. The Norks were playing chicken with their weapons—leaving parts of the world to wonder if they were one button away from a skin-melting death. China was talking out both sides of their mouth, refusing to commit to one side or the other. Russia was playing dumb about interfering with the election and their capabilities to hack our systems. If they'd done it once, they could do it again, this time with more dire consequences.

But had they? Had someone else? Is that what this was?

She'd be glad to get back home where she could discuss and debate her father and uncles on politics and what might really be happening. Her stepmom, Olivia, wouldn't discuss the president or anything political. She lived in a world of unicorns and rainbows. But her Aunt Gabby was always good for bouncing things off of, or having a calm and intelligent debate with.

Her breath was wasted on Becky and the guys down the hall. They were blithering idiots.

She was better on her own.

But without someone who knew how to read a compass, she realized she needed to take the quickest route, one that she knew well frontward and backward.

The interstate.

Home was a little more than an hour away by car, at normal speed.

Graysie grabbed her gun and tucked it into the back of her pants, stowed the ammo in her backpack, waved goodbye to a still-sleeping Becky, and ran down the two flights of stairs to the security guard's desk.

"I'm leaving."

The guard looked up, blinking rapidly at Graysie.

She'd interrupted his nap.

He cleared his throat and stood. "The administration said—"

"—I don't give a rat's ass what the administration said. I'm nineteen years old. If I don't need their permission to have a baby, buy a pack of smokes, join the army, or be shipped over to be shot by our enemies overseas, I sure as hell don't need their permission to go home. To *my* home, where I'm safe with my father."

Graysie flipped her long red hair behind her shoulder and stood tall and defiant—or as tall as her five feet five allowed—her lips pursed and her green eyes glaring at the nervous man.

"See here, young lady. It'll be dark soon. You need to—"

Graysie held up one finger. "No. *You* need to worry about what's going on right here under your nose. Upstairs, there's shit overflowing. There's parties going on in nearly all the suites. Underage drinking. Illegal drugs. Pills. *You* need to get the administration to look into that. And what about water? They've got three days to find water for all these kids before they reach a stage of dehydration that will need medical attention. If they're forcing us to stay here and you all aren't taking care of us, what's going to happen when our parents do arrive and their kids are sick...or worse? *That's* what you and the administration *need* to be worrying about."

She hiked her pack onto her shoulders and jangled her keys in the air. "I have transportation. I have a full tank of gas. And, I have protection." She turned and lifted up her shirt.

The guard gasped and backed up. He was stunned silent.

"I'm walking out of here and you can either radio someone to open the gate on the car park, or I'll drive right through it. Your choice, *Sir*."

She gave him a firm nod and walked out.

GABBY WAS ALREADY MAKING her way toward her sisters when she heard Olivia scream. They'd been gone too long. She broke into a run and slid to a stop at the edge of the clearing with her pistol ready.

She froze, barely believing her eyes.

On the outside of the small clearing stood three Harley Davidson motorcycles; one holding a pig. On the inside, her sisters were fighting—with bikers, no less.

Olivia was a flurry of knees, feet and elbows, trying to dislodge a mammoth of a man who held her from behind against his chest with heavily tattooed arms. He laughed at her pitiful struggling against his strength. She screamed, "Let me go!"

Five feet away Emma was a blur, turning in a half-circle, whipping a metal branding iron through the air back and forth between two very scary looking guys, one on each side of her. The two-foot long tool whistled as it arced, barely missing taking their nose off each time. As they ducked and dodged and laughed at her, grabbing at her clothes, she spit at them in fury.

A small Asian woman, mid-twenties, squatted in the middle of the mayhem on her knees, frantically trying to button her shirt with only one hand while holding her shirt shut with her other arm that ended at her wrist. She snatched up a small tattered purse from the ground, and held it close to her chest, shaking in fear.

And the pig wore a fancy skirt.

Was this even real?

She shook off her confusion and shot into the air.

It was deafening. Everyone froze.

Except the pig. The pig squealed and snorted, frantically twisting to try to free itself free from the strap that held it to the bike.

Everyone scattered.

Two of the men froze with their hands up and mouths open. Olivia and Emma broke free and rushed to stand behind Gabby. The man who'd held Olivia reached out for the Asian woman and shoved her behind him.

"What the hell is going on here?" Gabby screamed, once she had their attention.

Trunk, as his vest announced, wore a look of amused astonishment. "Damn. I thought you girls were joshing me. You really *did* have someone out there with a gun." He stared at Gabby, then back at Olivia. Then back to Gabby again.

He gave a long, slow smile.

"Hey boys, *look* what we have here..." He turned to them and winked. "Twins."

His crew hooted and hollered and pumped their fists into the air. "Worth more than a one-handed Asian on the list, Boss," one of them said. "We could *win* the hunt."

"Damn straight. As long as they're pretty, and there's *no denying that*," he said with a slow drawl, smiling ear to ear. He straightened up to stand taller and ran his hands down his vest as though to impress them, and took one step forward.

Gabby's hands trembled as she pointed the pistol directly at him. "Stop."

Trunk's smile slowly melted away.

Emma grabbed onto Olivia, gripping her shaking arm, and Olivia leaned in to Gabby. "Gabby, I wasn't *serious*...you can't just shoot him," she hissed in a loud whisper.

Trunk's charming smile was back. "Yeah, don't shoot me. Shit ain't that bad yet. There'd be lots of trouble for you over that." He spread his hands out, palms up. "Look, how 'bout we negotiate? You ladies ride with us, and she can go, if she wants." He jerked his thumb behind him, toward the young woman. "When we get back to the club, we'll tally up our points for the hunt. We'll feed you, pack you up with water, and then you can leave. I think we're going the opposite way you were heading—assuming you're going south if you're on this side of the interstate—but it's only an hour away. I'll even get these two to drive you home on their bikes." He jerked his head toward his crew who smiled suggestively at the girls.

Obviously, the dipshit couldn't do math; there were three of them. How would two get them home? Gabby spread her elbows, pushing her sisters back and took a firm stance, raising the gun higher. "I don't give a shit about your *hunt*. We're not going anywhere with you. Neither is she. Get her, Olivia."

Olivia hurried around Trunk to the young woman, who hung her head in shame. She and Olivia stepped back, farther away from Trunk, and circled back to stand behind Gabby and Emma.

Without warning, Gabby aimed and shot straight through the men. The women all flinched and covered their ears. The men hit the ground, screaming. Gabby shot twice more and her shots rang true. All that practice at the range was worth every hour.

All three bikes spewed air from their tires.

She pushed Emma and Olivia, shoving them back the way she'd come in. "Split up! You two go that way and get to the car. Drive south. We'll meet you a few miles down on the highway," she frantically whispered to her sisters. Grabbing the one available hand of the young woman, she took off the other way.

*G*abby's legs were jittery, her heart pumped wildly, and her backpack jiggled angrily against her spine, but they couldn't stop. If they did, they'd be found and there was no telling what kind of punishment would be doled out for not only stranding the bikers at the rest area, but robbing them of two—three? —of their winning prizes for their stupid scavenger hunt.

At least she'd left them the pig.

The young woman, who said her name was Mei, had tightly held her purse and run straight onto a deer trail that threaded through the woods on the backside of the rest area. Gabby had followed, but soon took the lead. They'd ran on the trail as far as it took them until it had ended with an army of tall trees, each looking dark and sinister, their trunks blocking out the sun.

They fought with every step, as gnarled and twisted branches caught at their clothes. Gabby felt like if they could cut through the dense woods, they'd be able to easily circle back to the interstate, where hopefully Larry and her sisters would find them.

If they were going the right way.

She wasn't sure, but she thought she heard at least one of the bikers somewhere behind them. This had turned into a very long game of hide-and-seek, and she was tired of playing.

What to do with Mei when we find Larry?

That question had been flipping and flopping around in her mind, along with false starts to a dozen different plans. They could probably squeeze Mei into the car, but did she really want to take her home? The girl looked like a prostitute, and had tell-tale marks of drug use.

Gabby couldn't stand drugs. When it came to drug users, she gave no quarter. Everyone had choices and she

gave no sympathy to people who made that particular
choice.

Mei was probably high now. That would explain why
she paid the seeping burn on her arm no attention. Gabby's
stomach rolled every time she looked at it. Grayson
wouldn't be too happy at them dragging this one in; one
more mouth to feed and probably nothing but trouble.

But she couldn't just leave her with the bikers. The girl
was barely older than Grayson and Olivia's daughter,
Graysie. Hardly more than a child. She needed their help in
more ways than one. What if the drugs came after the
abuse she was enduring? What if it was the bikers who'd
given her the drugs? Maybe she wasn't a regular user.
Women in abusive situations did crazy things.

Gabby and her sisters had all been through hell at one
time. Before meeting their forever husbands, each of them
had dealt with some sort of abuse in their lives. They were
stronger now, and one thing they'd all learned was to never
believe someone *wanted* to be in the bad position that they
were in. Sometimes a person just didn't know how to take
the first step to change their own journey. They needed
support and a hand up. Most of the time if you gave them
that hand, they'd grab it.

Gabby laughed out loud.

Mei needed more than *one* hand.

Stop it, she chided herself.

She was sliding into a terror-fueled hysteria. She was
tired, afraid, and possibly lost. Her legs were nearly give
out, twitchy and rubbery.

"Let's slow down, Mei." Gabby slowed to a fast walk and continued to plod along, her feet feeling heavier and heavier.

Mei gave her a grateful look. She'd been dragging, too, barely keeping up with Gabby.

Gabby was panting. *I'd kill for a cold bottle of water,* she thought and then shivered, realizing that wasn't even funny in these circumstances, even if she hadn't said it out loud.

She *had* thought about killing those men. She realized that somewhere deep inside of her, she was capable of it, too. For a moment, she wasn't looking at the biker in the woods. She was looking at a man from her past. A man who'd nearly forced her to take her own life. He was a monster, just like the bikers. Did killing a monster make her a monster, too?

She hoped she'd never find out.

They stopped to lean against a tree to rest. Mei stared worriedly behind them.

Gabby breathed silently, although it was an effort, and her lungs were seriously getting pissed from the abuse. She didn't want Mei to know just how worn out—and scared—she really was. Sweat dripped off her nose, hitting the dry leaves with an exaggerated *plop*. There were no other sounds, other than the distant tree frogs and cicadas. She listened harder. A breeze rustled up some leaves, but when it quieted, she heard nothing again.

The near silence was deafening.

She waved a hand at Mei and they slowly trudged forward another fifty feet.

Finally, through the trees she, she saw daylight and a glimpse of the highway covered in cars that had given up their fight and now lay haphazardly parked in two sleeping lines. There wasn't a person to be seen.

Until there was.

Larry's car came into sight, barreling down a clear gap and then swerving to zoom down the shoulder of the highway. He slid to a stop beside the two rows of gridlocked stalled cars, throwing up loose asphalt.

Gabby's heart leapt. They'd found them!

But how? Can they see us? Through the trees?

She watched him jump out of the car and stomp to the other side.

What is he doing?

"Hey! We're here!" she screamed, pushing the brush and branches out of her way, trying to break free of the forest to step out onto the road.

She heard Olivia and Emma yelling, but couldn't make out their words.

Why is no one looking at me and Mei? Maybe they haven't seen us?

Starting to panic, she hurried, walking faster and trying to break into a run. Maybe they were out of gas, too? Maybe the bikers were coming? Had they found a way to fix their tires? Were they right behind them?

Gabby looked to the left but could only see more stranded cars and now, a small group of people were walking a few miles back, no bigger than toy soldiers from this distance.

A stitch in her side struck her suddenly and she bent over in pain. "Run, Mei! Catch them!"

She stared through the trees as Mei pushed harder, opening a bigger space through the limbs and leaves. Now Gabby could see Larry. H was in a rage, throwing their make-shift T-shirt bags out of his car.

He was dumping them.

Asshole!

All other thoughts flew from her mind as the belief planted itself firmly that they'd be stranded, hours and hours away from home, on foot. The bikers would find them soon. They'd be taken to some *Sons of Anarchy-type* clubhouse and forced to be Old Ladies.

She may never see Jake again.

Or worse.

She stood stooped over, with one hand clutching her side, paralyzed with fear. It all caught up with her. She was tired of being the one always in charge. Tired of Olivia being so flaky and undependable. Tired of Emma being so invisibly quiet except when she was being the peacemaker. She couldn't handle the pressure. All she wanted was to get herself and her sisters home safely. But she'd screwed up *everything* so far.

She leaned farther over, grabbing her knees. She couldn't breathe.

Her bag slid up and hit her in the back of the head. The sweat that soaked her clothes turned into a prickly bath of ice water. She turned her head up just in time to see Larry get back in the car, and leave Olivia and Emma standing

still on the side of the road, shoulders slumped, their bags
at their feet.

Probably waiting on Gabby—or someone—to tell them
what to do next.

To hell with it.

She was done.

They were on their own. She couldn't be the boss
anymore. She sucked at it and had only got her sisters into
a bigger mess than they were in at the beach resort. Olivia
should be stepping up; it was her husband after all that was
the prepper. With their elderly father now living out of
town with his fiancé, Grayson was sort of the new family
patriarch. Didn't that make *Olivia* the matriarch? Surely,
she learned *something* from Grayson.

She swallowed past a lump in her throat and stood up
straight. Mei had stopped, waiting as though in limbo
between Gabby and her sisters out on the road. Gabby was
ready to explode.

Furiously looking around, she stalked over to an abandoned bike dumped in the ditch. She got on the bike and
turned it the opposite way, calling out behind her, "Go.
Walk with them. I'm going on my own from here."

21

GABBY RANTED AND RAVED, throwing her fist into the air and then giving Larry a double one-finger salute to his rear-view mirror. She couldn't do it. She couldn't leave her sisters—and she'd left her bag. She'd meant to. They'd need it worse than her. But she wasn't so angry she didn't realize she needed it too.

She'd only ridden a minute up the road before turning around and pedaling back as fast as she could to try to catch Larry. But he was too far ahead.

He'd driven slowly away, leaving them stranded, answering her one-fingered salute with an obnoxious honk of his horn. She hoped the bikers found him.

"Piece of shit!" she screamed, straddling the bike.

She jumped off of it and let it fall to the ground and whipped around to her sisters. "Why'd he dump us?" she yelled.

Olivia backed away from her.

"Calm down, Gabby. It's not her fault," Emma answered. "He's a coward. When we told him about that gang, he said he didn't want to be caught with us."

Olivia held up her arm. "But look, I still have my Rolex. We can find someone else to trade with. Although I'd really like to keep it..."

Gabby rolled her eyes and clenched her jaw and turned, stomping back through the ditch to the tree-line where she'd dropped her bug-out bag. Mei stood beside the bag, silent and wary, staring at Gabby with guilt pinching her eyes.

"It's not your fault," Gabby muttered. "Come on."

Olivia tried to pick up the bike, dropping it on the first try. "Let's take this. We can take turns riding it," she said.

Gabby kept walking. "Fuck that bike."

She snatched her bag up with a heavy hand and trudged back to the road, stepping out in front of her sisters and leading the way.

Again.

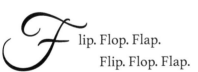

lip. Flop. Flap.

Flip. Flop. Flap.

The slapping of Olivia's flip-flops was driving everyone insane, on top of the waves of heat rolling up off the asphalt, giving more weight to the feeling of being in hell. To her credit, Olivia had run like the wind earlier in them, but now they were nearly destroyed, the rubber almost completely melted on the soles. Gabby watched as Olivia exhaustedly measured each step while looking down and gripping the stubborn piece between her toes that barely held the shoes together. Her toes were bunched up, crooked and strained, and when she raised her feet, there was a gaping hole in the bottom of each shoe, clearly showing the dirt on Olivia's feet.

That's gonna leave a mark.

"Stop, Olivia," Gabby said, feeling guilty that in her rage she'd stupidly made Olivia leave the bike. She could have ridden it to save her feet some grief.

Olivia didn't argue. She stepped off the road to the ditch and heavily sat down, stripping off her shoes and rubbing her feet.

Gabby dug through her bug-out bag. "There's *got* to be something in here to fix them."

She found a pencil, wrapped in layers of silver duct tape. "Aha!" Silently, she thanked her husband for listening to Grayson and packing her a bug-out bag. She'd meant to do it herself, but never got around to it. Jake had done well. Quickly she focused on the flip-flops before thoughts of Jake crippled her.

She wound the duct tape around Olivia's shoes multiple times, covering the holes and giving her more padding to replace what had melted or been worn away. She handed them back to Olivia, not even earning a thank you.

She sighed.

After an hour of arguing, her sisters—and Mei—had lost the fight, and they were sulking. They wanted to step off the interstate, and cut through the country, hoping to get away from the energy-depleting heat and into some shade, and shave time off their long walk home.

But someone had dropped the map.

Gabby cringed again. She'd let Olivia believe it was her, having left it in the car when they'd first arrived at the rest area. But actually, Gabby had picked up the map and the picture of her and Olivia standing in front of Jake's truck and had put them in her back pocket before their snafu in the woods with the bikers.

Gabby had left the bike. And *Gabby* had lost the map. *And* the picture. Three screw-ups. Maybe more... And without the map, she couldn't be sure they'd find their way home if they left the interstate.

But the girls had another point, too. If and when the bikers fixed their tires, they could be right behind them. They'd hedged their bets, planning to run and hide if they heard motorcycles, and so far, they hadn't. But their luck had to run out sometime. They would be harder to find if they took a shortcut and got off of the highway. But, they were all directionally-challenged and relied far too much on the modern conveniences of google maps and GPS's. She didn't trust them to find their own way home without that map, which had their route highlighted all the way to the homestead.

She watched as they shared a last bottle of water, passing it around between the three of them. Finally, Mei handed it to her.

Gabby shook her head.

Penance for her unspoken crimes.

Let them have it.

"Okay, I give. Let's get off the road."

---

*A*s night began to fall around them, their hearts fell with it. At this point, after hours of walking, they had no idea how close or far from home they were. They'd lost sight of the interstate long ago and only hoped they were still walking the right direction.

Mei was in the front now, where they could prod her along and keep an eye on her. Although they didn't know exactly how old she was, Gabby felt sure she was very young. Mei should be stronger than all of them, not weaker. She had been through a lot, but in the past few hours she had *really* slowed down, and even more worrying, she was convinced they didn't want her there, and didn't want her to come home with them. Repeatedly, she'd offered to just go it alone and head a different direction.

At this point, Gabby could admit to herself, she *didn't* want her there. She had a feeling Mei had some very serious issues. But Mei had said she had no one and nowhere else to go, so Gabby kept her mouth shut when Olivia and Emma stepped in to reassure her she was wanted.

Mei stopped walking and cocked her head, and rubbed her red, itchy eyes for the thousandth time. Gabby hoped she wasn't going to dig through that purse again. She'd stopped and dug through the small bag a dozen times already, never finding what she was looking for.

"Look," Mei yelled excitedly. "A creek!"

Gabby raised an eyebrow. She was hesitant to believe Mei. Twice now Mei had seen something that wasn't there. She'd freaked out over sticks on the trail, screaming and jumping around like a lunatic, thinking they were snakes, startling all of them.

They weren't.

But this time, it was real. Gabby could hear the sound of water bubbling. Finding a burst of energy, the girls ran forward. They all jumped in to the ankle-deep water of the narrow creek, splashing it onto their faces and each other.

"Can we drink it?" Olivia asked.

They'd been without water for hours.

They all looked at Gabby. If someone was going to be a party pooper, it'd be her.

"Let's filter it first," Gabby suggested. "I don't think anyone wants to be shitting like a goose while squatting on the ground."

Olivia scrunched her nose up at her sister's bad language. As Gabby's patience wore thin, her mouth always got nasty, and her own filter soon would be totally gone. She'd always been that way, and Olivia had always chided her for it.

Gabby dug through her backpack and pulled out a sandwich baggie that held a Sawyer Mini filter kit. She unrolled the bladder and blew into it and held it down in the stream until it filled up. She screwed the filter onto the bladder, and handed it to Olivia first; she seemed to need water the worst.

Olivia held it in her hand and then looked at Gabby. "Do I drink the whole thing?"

"No. Take what you need right now and pass it around."

Olivia scrunched up her nose. "So we're all going to be drinking after each other?"

Gabby sighed. "Yeah, Olivia. Because *you* left the other bags at home, this is the only filter we have. That's on you. Gotta share now."

Indignantly, she drank long and deep and then tried to pass it to Gabby. She waved it on to Emma and Mei first. After the first bag was gone, Gabby filled it up again. They split two energy bars, surprised to still find they had some, and then emptied the bladder, drinking as much as they could hold. Three more times they filled it up and drank until they squeezed out the last drop, and finally the last bag was filtered into the empty water bottle for later.

Twice, while they were eating, drinking, and resting, Emma had tried to bring up their father. Neither Olivia nor Gabby wanted to discuss their dad. Getting home seemed such a challenge already, and he was another two hours away from Grayson and Olivia's homestead, now living in Anderson, South Carolina, where he'd moved with his fiancé. They were getting on in years and there was no way they'd attempt to make it to the homestead; that they knew, so eventually if the power didn't come back on, they'd have to make a plan to go get them.

But for now, one problem at a time.

The women got very quiet.

Gabby couldn't think past seeing her husband, Jake. He'd not been himself lately and she wondered if he was suffering from some sort of depression. He wouldn't talk about it with her. She hoped he'd gone to Grayson's as soon as the grid went down so at least he wouldn't be alone.

Olivia was worried beyond belief about her husband, Grayson, and her stepdaughter, Graysie—not to mention her dog, Ozzie. Graysie was away at college an hour from home. Surely, she left before the gas was gone and the roads were gridlocked, but what if she didn't?

And Emma didn't dare mention her son Rickey, or her own husband, Dusty. She couldn't even whisper their names for fear of breaking down. With Dusty's job, he could be in more danger than all of them, and Rickey could be right in the middle of it with him.

Mei wasn't interested in talking either. She went from sitting to standing to pacing in equal measure, driving them all insane with her inability to sit still for a moment.

Gabby packed everything away and stood up. "Let's go."

They'd lost a lot of time sitting next to the creek, but left with a little more oomph and one refilled water bottle. Now they were in near pitch darkness struggling through a stand of thick forest in single file. Finally, they found a small trail but had no idea how far it went. They could be in here all night.

Gabby ran straight into a branch and leapt back just before it gouged her eye out. "I think we need to turn around," she said.

"No way. We've been in here almost an hour now. I'm not going all that way back," Olivia answered. Olivia thought they were close to home. She was wrong...Gabby just knew it. It didn't feel like home yet. Or anywhere near it.

She gave in. "Okay, but I've got to pee. You all go on without me, I'll catch up in a minute."

"You sure?" Olivia asked. "Aren't you scared?"

Gabby shook her head, although not sure if Olivia could see her. "I've got the gun, remember? I'll only be a minute. Just keep walking." She was afraid if they stopped and sat down, they wouldn't get back up.

The moon chose that moment to shine through the clouds and trees, throwing a patch of light onto the trail as Olivia, Emma and Mei slowly walked on.

Gabby stumbled around trying to find the perfect tree to squat in front of; a big one to lean against if she lost her balance, with a small one to hang onto next to it, hopefully with a patch of higher ground that would drain the pee *away* from her shoes; not on them.

Finally, she dropped her pack, removed the gun from the back of her pants, and hunkered down. As she emptied her bladder she wondered what kind of trail this was... a deer trail? A 4-wheeler trail?

It didn't take her long to find out.

In a moment, a baby pig ran across the trail, and then turned and zigzagged back the way it'd come, nearly running right over Gabby's feet.

Gabby gasped and froze, waiting to see if it came back.

Her first thought was the bikers had found them, but this pig wasn't wearing a skirt, and it wasn't white. It was spotted gray and black.

It was a wild piglet.

And where there was a baby, there'd be a mama close.

She jerked her pants up in a hurry so she could warn her sisters.

Too late.

A piercing scream cut through Gabby's heart and the woods came alive with the sound of running, squealing and snorting.

Gabby cupped her hands to her mouth and screamed, "Climb a tree!"

There was no way anyone could outrun a wild hog in the dark woods.

Her heart pounded as she gripped the pistol with one hand and blocked the branches from her face with the other. She flew down the trail guided by the tiniest bit of moonlight, feeling her skin being slapped and ripped with a torrent of limbs.

It's going to kill them. It probably has tusks. I should have stayed with them. I'm the one with the gun... She could just see her sisters smeared with blood, laying in dripping heaps while wild animals gnawed at them. Her life would never be the same. Losing her twin sister would be like losing a limb. Losing both her sisters would be worse than death.

She shrieked again, loud and long, and raced after them. "*No! No! No!*" Blindly, she raced through the dark woods with one arm out in front of her, slapping away the branches and brush. Here, the trees were spread apart more.

"Don't run! It'll catch you!" she screamed, knowing they probably couldn't hear her.

Climb a tree Climb a tree Climb a tree

That was the last thought she had before darkness over took her.

22

GABBY PATTED the bandage on her head and silently thanked her husband once more. She promised herself if they made it home, she'd pay more attention to the details of prepping, and less attention to her passion for shooting. Now she realized there was more to being prepared than learning how to shoot a gun and spending time at the range. She and her sisters were barely more prepared than the average sheeple—as Grayson called them.

Quickly she thought about all their mistakes so far. None of them had the right clothes for an emergency hike down the road; they were wearing summer shorts for Pete's sake. Olivia didn't have *any* walking shoes. They had one small bug-out bag. More of a Get-Home bag really. She wasn't familiar with what was *in* that bag beforehand. Everything should have been tested before an emergency. She wasn't even sure if the Sawyer filter had ever been used before or if they'd done it right—were they supposed to clean it before using it? Was she supposed to use another filter before drinking it? Filter it twice? She had no idea; she'd faked it earlier because she was too thirsty to figure it out. It was still possible they could all end up squatting for hours later for all she knew. And that would be her fault, too. Also, they hadn't kept the gas tank topped off. She was sure there were many more mistakes and Grayson would be sorely disappointed in all of them before it was over.

She was just thankful her other half had been listening to Grayson when he stressed the importance of an emergency pack. Jake didn't care much for shooting, but he'd obviously took the whole prepping thing more serious than she had. He'd come through in the end as the half of their marriage that saved the day, just by packing that small bag.

The first aid kit had come in handy again, especially the sterile alcohol wipes, antibiotic cream, and the roll of bandage. When she'd first opened her eyes to find Olivia, Emma and Mei staring at her, she'd forgotten where she was, and who the strange Asian girl was. It'd taken her a minute to assure herself she wasn't dreaming. Her sisters were alive, well, and in one piece. She took another few minutes to get on her feet and find her bearings.

The sow had run right past her sisters, who'd heard it— or something—coming and had all jumped up on a huge rock, clutching each other. They'd watched it run past in a blur followed by a litter of babies. They'd called out to Gabby that they were okay but in her frenzied state, she hadn't heard them.

She'd flown through the trail directly into disaster, tripping over a root and knocking herself out. Now she and Olivia would be twins again, both having nearly identical cuts and bumps on their heads.

They'd also put salve on Mei's burn and wrapped it, much to her indifference.

Back on the trail nearly an hour now, they were exhausted. They'd all *thought* they were in great shape with their hot yoga, exercise dance classes, and daily walks. But the uneven terrain and long, steady pace was different than flittering around on a gym floor or walking through the neighborhood.

Their ankles, feet, and hips ached. Their arms and legs were scratched and bleeding. Gabby's lungs felt abused and even her hands hurt; they stung where she'd stumbled several times since knocking herself out, falling and catching herself on her hands in the dark. Her balance was gone. Her head swam with pain. She and Olivia probably both had concussions.

The sow had badly spooked them and slowed their pace by more than half. None of them knew anything about wild hogs. Would it chase them? Would it hunt them? They'd all seen stories of wild boar getting up to three hundred pounds and running thirty miles per hour. But regardless of their fear, they had to keep moving. To keep the fear at bay, they whispered while they walked. Mostly about what was in those other two bug-out bags back at Grayson and Olivia's house... more water? A tent? A sleeping bag?

If only Olivia hadn't taken them out of the car, they

might be setting up a camp right now to lay down and have a rest.

In Gabby's bag, they had found cinnamon candies to suck on while digging for first aid supplies, and they'd eaten nearly the whole bag as they walked, giving them some vigor, as well as fixing their stale breath, and keeping their hunger at bay.

Quietly, they crept through the woods. A few steps... then stop. Listen. More walking...then stopping...listening to be sure nothing was chasing them. When they thought they heard a noise behind them, they'd run like hell until they were far beyond or in front of it.

It was an on again, off again merry-go-round of panic, especially for Mei.

Finally, they were out of the woods and were on open ground. The clouds had cleared to allow the full moon the stage, giving them more light than they'd seen in hours.

Gabby ignored the begging to stop for the night until she too couldn't take another step. She dropped her pack and flopped to the ground, leaning against the trunk of a lone tree in exhaustion.

"My feet," Olivia said in a rush of breath, joining her on the ground. "I don't think I'll be able to walk again tomorrow, Gabby. They hurt."

"You can. You will. We don't have a choice."

Seriously?

What did Olivia think Gabby and Emma's feet felt like? Or Mei's? Even with a well-fitted, broken-in pair of running shoes, Gabby's feet ached so badly that she wasn't even sure it was pain anymore. The pleasure of getting off of them conflicted with the ache from walking, making her giddy with relief. But her rest was short-lived. She had to get up again, keep moving. Or she'd be done for the night.

They needed a fire. A real fire this time. It was too spooky out here to sleep in the dark, and a fire might keep predators away. *She hoped.*

Sighing, she pulled herself up to scrape out a spot, while Emma attempted to gather branches for kindling.

"I'll help. Just give me a minute," Olivia offered. Gabby looked at her sister, seeing more than pain on her face. Olivia was exhausted. She was clearly weaker than anyone in the group and she'd walked, and ran, all this way in faulty flip-flops, and her feet looked really bad for it. Even in the moonlight, Gabby could see they were crisscrossed in bloody scratches from their trek through the woods.

"No, we got it. You take it easy."

Olivia didn't put up an argument. Instead, she pulled off her shoes and rubbed her feet. Emma wandered close by, gathering twigs, and muttering about hating squats as she struggled to dip and bend to pick up each stick. She was in better shape than any of them, yet she too was ready to drop. They were all hot, tired and cranky.

Mei seemed to wander around in a circle, not doing much of anything except shaking, muttering and scratching at her arms—even the one without the newly-burned brand. Finally, Gabby saw her pull something from her small purse and continue her pacing.

As Mei passed by, Gabby caught a glimpse in the moonlight. It was a picture of a little girl no more than one year old. Tiny black pigtails with red ribbons adorned her head and she proudly displayed dimples next to a nearly tooth-less smile.

"Who's that, Mei? Is that your little girl?" Gabby asked.

Mei stopped and held the picture up to her face, staring as though she'd never seen it before. She muttered something incoherent and walked away, mumbling to herself.

Gabby exchanged concerned looks with her sisters and they let it go.

Ten minutes later, Gabby was squatting next to the small pile of kindling. Emma didn't find much. The tree they were under seemed to be the only tree nearby. Every-thing was green, and they were afraid to move out too far. Each piece they'd found had been hard-earned and their fire wouldn't be lasting long. Gabby carefully stacked them and struck the lighter repeatedly.

The fire wouldn't take hold.

She cursed, and tried again and again. She cussed and sucked her tender thumb. The lighter was too hot. She changed hands and struck it again. Still, no fire.

Emma and Olivia sat quietly watching her. They didn't have much experience with campfires either. The guys always took care of that. Mei sat off by herself with her arms wrapped around her bent knees, rocking and humming to music only she could hear, apparently.

In exasperation, Gabby snatched her backpack. She furiously dug through it, looking for something—anything

—to burn better. She pulled out a stretchy band with a square attached to it.

"Omigod. Look!"

It was a headlamp.

They'd walked all this way through the woods and the night, stumbling blindly, and all this time there'd been a flashlight. She rolled her eyes at her stupidity.

Clearly, they needed to take the time to *really* go through her pack.

She dug further and found a prescription bottle. Turning on the head lamp, she read the word "fire" written in red Sharpie around it. She turned it and read the rest of the word, "...starter."

The bottle contained sticky cotton balls. Gabby smelled one and smiled. "Petroleum jelly," she told the girls. She tucked one under the tinder and struck the lighter again.

It lit.

She looked up with a smile. "Who's cooking? I started the fire."

Olivia's deadpan face told Gabby she'd rather go hungry than attempt to drum up enough energy to cook. And Emma didn't cook, even in the best of times. Mei looked down at her feet.

"What are we going to cook over?" Emma asked.

"The fire," Gabby answered. "Duh."

"No, I mean, we don't have a rack. Only a cup. You going to just stick it in the fire?"

Gabby dropped her head. Emma was right. She hadn't even thought about it. There was probably some super-simple way to rig up a rack to hang the cup from, or set the cup on over the fire, but she didn't have the brainpower to figure it out this late. *Another thing we aren't prepared for.*

She sighed and pulled out a tiny rocket stove. "Here, start a tiny fire in this, too." She handed it to Emma. It was lightweight and only big enough to hold one cup, but one cup was all they had anyway. "You'll need some small twigs or pinecones. You can break them up and stick them in there to burn. We still needed a campfire out here though. It's too dark."

While Emma attempted to put the little stove together with light from the campfire, Gabby dug again into the backpack. "Okay, there's two pouches of Mountain House Freeze-dried meals. We've got chili mac with beef or lasagna. I can't handle either one of these without access to a bathroom. Thanks, Jake," she grumbled. "Oh wait, here's an envelope of Lipton noodle soup mix. That's only enough for one of—"

"—then you better shut up before you end up having to feed the whole damn neighborhood," a deep, gruff voice interrupted.

Gabby threw herself backward, landing on her rump in the dirt and scooting away from the voice—also scooting away from her gun that she'd taken out of her pants so she could relax against the tree for a moment.

"Who the hell are you?" she yelled.

Olivia and Emma scrambled in a crabwalk across the grass the few feet they needed to get to Gabby, where they all huddled together.

Mei froze in place, staring up at the stranger with an open mouth.

"I'd ask you the same, but I don't give a damn. I'd have just rolled over and gone to sleep, except the missus insisted I come out here and check on you girls."

"Missus?" Gabby asked in confusion. "Where is she? Where did you come from? What do you want?"

"From the farmhouse, just across the field over there," he said as he pointed into the darkness. "Voices travel out here, especially now that the lights are out. I heard y'all as soon as you stepped into my field. You need to work on your sneak-skills."

"We weren't sneaking. We didn't know we were in your field. We didn't know we were even *in* a field. We'll leave," Gabby snapped. She stared the old man in the eye, after appraising his overalls, rubber boots fit for chicken-coop poop-scooping and John Deere cap. The bill was bent and frayed and short tufts of white hair stuck out the sides.

Regardless of his age, he was strong. His broad shoulders framed a rather fit looking torso, and his arms were corded with hard-earned muscle. He wore a red T-shirt under his overalls and Gabby could just make out the acronym: MAGA.

Make America Great Again.

His wrinkled face scowled through the scraggly lines and whiskers. He didn't look the friendly sort.

With a big foot and a frustrated kick, he sent dirt over their fire, immediately squashing it. "Not only are you too loud, but you're advertising your spot out here with this fire. I can't leave you girls out here tonight. The missus won't let me. She's afraid something is gonna get ya, and trust me, there's plenty of varmints out here tonight that would *and* could."

A chill ran down Gabby's spine. She couldn't see much past six feet with the limited moonlight. Was someone—or something—watching them now?

The old man jerked his head toward the direction he'd appeared from. "Come with me. I'd rather deal with three whining city girls than deal with y'all's dead bodies and told-you-so's from the wife in the morn'. You girls can sleep in the house tonight."

He stomped off, fully expecting them to follow.

They didn't disappoint him.

23

GRAYSIE RAN her tongue over her gritty teeth and revved her engine. She drummed her fingers on the steering wheel. No one had come to let her out of the car parking lot; the gates were still closed. Eventually, she'd fallen asleep and slept all night and half the morning. She should've been sleeping in her car since the power went out. Smelled better out here and she felt safe cocooned in Sally.

But she was still stuck. The only way to get out of here now was to drive through the gate.

She shrugged. She'd seen it on TV a million times. She could do this.

She centered her car up in front of the gap and stepped on the gas, gaining a lot of speed in a short amount of pavement and barreling toward the small opening between the gates. Her dad was going to kill her when he saw Sally—her car. This was definitely going to leave a mark, as he liked to say.

She sped the short distance and at the last minute squinted her eyes. "Gird your loins, girl," she whispered, again, something else her daddy liked to say.

Metal screamed and Graysie flinched, waiting for her seatbelt to slam into her as her car was ripped to a stop.

But it didn't.

In complete astonishment to her, she actually did it! The mustang rammed through the gates, throwing them wide open, but leaving them bent as they waved and bounced back in fury. She gave her best rebel yell as she braked heavily to make the turn and screeched around the corner.

Her spirits lifted. Home was only a little over an hour away. If she'd made it this far, she could make it there alone. She'd be there soon.

To her surprise, it was clear all the way to the interstate and down the access ramp to I-77. If she didn't know any better, she'd think the college administration had made everything up. Other than no moving traffic, everything looked normal.

So far.

But once on the interstate, she ran into problems only minutes later. She was coming up on both lanes mostly blocked by stalled cars. Some were wrecked into the others. As she got closer she saw there was an opening, but a crowd of people were walking, blocking the one clear side of the road.

Hearing her engine, they turned as one and watched her approach. She slowed when she was within fifty feet of them and grabbed her gun that she'd laid in the seat beside her. Slowly, she rolled up to them and beeped the horn.

The bulk of the crowd moved to the side, but three men stood their ground, one holding his hand up in the air in a 'stop' motion, and the other two waving their arms.

Graysie rolled her window all the way up and creeped forward a bit further.

"Get out of the way," she yelled through the windshield, sure they could hear her or at least get the point, punctuated by her brandishing her gun back at them.

The two guys who were waving dove out of her way without need of a second warning. The third guy ran toward the car, weaving around the front to run toward her door. He was dirty and desperate, and not someone she would have stopped for even in the best of circumstances.

Her heart bounced in fear as she goosed the gas and left him standing there chasing wind.

She breathed a sigh of relief when the road was mostly clear for the next ten miles, other than a few stragglers walking in groups of two or three, who didn't have the energy to try to stop her. They merely moved aside when they heard her coming, not even bothering to turn around. She slowed when passing them and glanced at their hopeless gait, then sped up a long hill, gaining speed all the way toward a bridge that crossed the river.

The top of the bridge disappeared as the hill grew steeper before it crossed the water and she hoped it was clear on the other side. If she maintained this sort of speed, she'd be home tonight. She could've kicked herself for not leaving days ago. She could've been home right now.

Her mind drifted to home as the road bent out of sight ahead, arcing into the sky.

She could barely wait to see her dad, and Ozzie. Her entire family would be a welcome sight. Hopefully, her dad knew what was going on; why the phones weren't working and the power wasn't back on yet. She swallowed hard as she realized he may have news that she didn't want to hear.

The road in front of her disappeared into the remains of a blue sky as she zoomed closer to topping the hill. Her visibility was abruptly cut off at the top of the bridge. She held her breath, hoping her luck hadn't run out.

It had.

The road wasn't clear.

A wall of stalled and wrecked vehicles blocked it.

She slammed on her brakes, and veered right toward the low concrete wall. She could barely see the river at the bottom of a huge drop-off. She'd never make that fall. She jerked the wheel to the left, all while in a long, screaming slide, and then realized there was nothing to keep her from falling off that side either. She corrected and watched the wall of metal quickly approaching her windshield as she steered right into it, standing on her brakes.

Omigod. Stop Stop Stop

Her prayer went unanswered as metal connected with metal. Everything slowed down. Graysie felt her seatbelt cut into her as her hair flew past her face, long tendrils reaching desperately toward the windshield. Out of the corner of her eye and through the red veil of hair, she saw her gun slide into the floor in slow motion. The sound was deafening; the loudest thing she'd heard in days. It seemed to go on and on as she wondered if that was her...*her car*, making that sound. She felt as though her heart had stopped, along with time, as she waited an eternity to come full stop, anticipating a head-on collision of her face with the steering wheel. Seconds seemed like minutes...

Her head was thrown forward, but then jerked backward as she finally roared to a noisy stop followed by dead silence—other than a strange hissing noise.

Thank you, seatbelt.

Her vision was a blur of white. The sudden stop was punctuated with a crash of something falling onto the pavement beneath her car, probably something under the hood that was now kissing the back of a very tired and abandoned Volvo, and the loud pop of her airbag. She rested her head against the bag that saved her, breathing hard.

The bag deflated on it's own, laying limp against the steering wheel. After reassuring herself she was okay, other than probably two black eyes and a few bruises, she put her car in reverse and tried to back up.

It wasn't going anywhere.

The car door squealed in fury as she pushed it open. She got out and stood still a moment, waiting for the pain to come. When none did, she stretched her arms and legs, and wiggled her fingers. She was okay—but she knew major pain would come later. She walked to the front. The collision had married her Mustang to the Volvo. It would take a tow truck, at least, to separate them. Maybe even the Jaws of Life.

The sun was slipping away. It'd be dark within minutes. A small crowd of figures were making their way up the bridge now. *Maybe someone to walk with?*

In her head, she heard her father's voice contradicting her own.

No.

Run.

She reached into the car, and grabbed her gun and her bag, furiously digging around until she found the hat her father had packed her. She twisted her long red hair and pulled it up, shoving the hat on top of it, and started walking at as fast a pace as the heavy backpack would allow. There was no time to unpack it now and leave anything behind. Besides, she wasn't sure what she might need later.

Much later—Graysie had no concept of time and didn't have a watch—after miles of walking, she could see the sign for her exit. Feeling a rush of gratitude, she found the energy to run again at a slow pace, with her heavy backpack trying to drag her down with every step. She wore out quicker than she thought she would've and within minutes was huffing and puffing, her shoulders screaming in agony from the extra weight. She should have listened to her dad when in his note he said to empty the bag of anything she wouldn't need.

But again, how was she to know what wasn't needed?

He'd always said better to have it and not need it, than to need it and not have it.

The road off the interstate seemed darker. Everything looked different—unfamiliar—on foot. A cloud of smoke hung in the air. Creepy. The best she could figure, home was at least an hour's walk through the country. She needed to rest, if only for a little while.

She came around a bend and saw a somewhat familiar barn. Probably familiar because the last two she'd passed looked just like it in the dark. A farmhouse was farther down the dirt road and she couldn't see or hear anyone. It seemed to be the perfect place to rest up and if she wasn't mistaken about where she was, she could cut across the fields and through the woods, and she thought it would put her out on her father's land and trim at least five miles off her journey, but it would be a hike.

And it would be darker and scarier.

Her pulse had been going way too strong for the past hour. She gripped her gun tightly in her hand. She'd let her fear of the dark get to her and build and build until it was nearly unmanageable. This was the closest to a panic attack she'd had since the day her mother drowned years ago in the aftermath of a hurricane, when she'd sacrificed herself for her daughter.

She couldn't go there. She had to stop her mind from rolling into that.

Pull yourself together, Graysie, she told herself. Again, she jerked on the straps of her backpack, hopping a little to try to re-situate the heavy bag. Her back and shoulders were begging for a rest.

She decided to stop in the shelter of the barn, if it was empty, and rest. Then she'd be ready to walk home. She'd be in her own bed tonight, safe under her dad's roof.

PUCK ARRIVED BRIGHT AND EARLY, knocking on Grayson's door.

"Mr. Gray Man!"

Ozzie jumped off the bed, barking with delight, and scratched at the door.

Grayson stumbled around trying to get his pants on and led Ozzie out. He rubbed his eyes and blinked in the bright sunlight. Trying not to sound too irritated in spite of another nearly sleepless night worrying about his family, he asked. "What are you doing here so early, Puck?"

"I wanted to see if Ozzie could come out and play," Puck muttered in a small voice, and then dropped his head. He blindly held a can up in the air. "And I brought breakfast if you can open it."

Grayson took in a deep breath, and then sighed it out. He'd forgotten to show the boy how to use a can opener.

"I'll be out in a few minutes." He left Ozzie out to play with the kid.

Half an hour and half a pot of coffee later, Grayson emerged outside with a better attitude. At least the boy would keep his mind off of Olivia and Graysie, and he could do with a little help around the homestead, too.

Ignoring Puck's contribution to breakfast, he fried them some Spam and eggs using a cast iron skillet on the grill. He watched with wonder and a little bit of disgust as Puck nearly inhaled everything in two minutes flat. At one point, he thought he'd have to intervene when Puck eyeballed Ozzie eating his own breakfast.

After eating, Grayson called Puck over to the porch. He held up a spoon and the can of ravioli that Puck had brought with him. "Okay. I'm going to show you how use a spoon to open this can, and then you can help me out around here a bit and earn that breakfast. Okay?"

Puck solemnly nodded.

After thinking about it, he realized someone may have already tried to teach Puck how to open a can with a hand-held can opener. While most people thought it was simple, he had seen other adults in his life that just couldn't get the hang of it, and kids definitely had trouble with. Kids couldn't open a can to save their life. He wasn't surprised Puck wasn't able to figure it out. But with the boy's strength, there was no way he *wouldn't* be able to do the spoon-trick he was about to show him, and as long as Puck could find a spoon, he'd always have way to open cans in an emergency.

He held up the spoon. "So, you grip the spoon real tight

in the palm of one hand, with about half of the round end sticking *out*. Then you hold the can tight with your other hand, and start sawing back and forth with your spoon around the top edge. It'll soften the metal. The longer you saw back and forth, the easier it will be to open." Grayson sawed with the spoon back and forth until his spoon pierced through the lid with a half-inch long crack.

He showed Puck the top of the can. "See that crack? You're in. Now you can either keep sawing around the whole circle of the can if you want to remove the entire lid, or you can poke your spoon through and sort of cut the top open. See there?" Grayson sawed at the hole, making it longer while Puck watched wide eyed.

"Then you can bend the top up and get to your food. But be careful, that jagged edge can give you a mean cut. It might be best for you to pour the food into a bowl or something. Don't ever eat out of the can, okay?" A cut from a can could get nasty, and without medical services running, or any hospitals open, it'd be best to avoid any injuries.

Puck nodded and took off at a run toward the picnic table where they'd eaten breakfast. He grabbed his dirty paper plate and ran back, holding it out to Grayson.

Grayson laughed. "You want to eat this? Now? You're still hungry?" He hoped Mama Dee had lots of cans in her pantry...

Puck dropped down on the ground beside Ozzie, reminding Grayson of when Graysie sat crisscross applesauce in kindergarten, and shoved the square raviolis into his mouth with his hands. He'd eat one, and then give

Ozzie one, sharing until they were all gone. He wiped the red messy sauce on his pant legs. *Olivia would have had a heart attack.*

Instead of getting up, he laid down with the dog, snuggling him close.

Grayson stood over him scratching his head. *Weird time for a lay-down.*

Suddenly he stood up like a jack-in-the-box. "Can I have some more water, Mr. Gray Man?"

"It's Gray*son*. But yeah, sure, kid."

The boy ran back to the table and turned up the half-full gallon of water Grayson had set out for their lunch, ignoring the paper cup he'd previously been using, drinking straight from the jug. *Another cringe-worthy moment.*

"Uh, you can just take that with you when you go home," Grayson said. He had a phobia about drinking after anyone other than his wife, Olivia.

Puck's eyes lit up. "Thank you!"

"How you doing on water at your house anyway?"

It hadn't even occurred to Grayson to ask before. It was hard for him to remember most people didn't put back water for *just in case* or emergencies. And with Puck's mom having been gone when the power went off, he seriously doubted the boy would have known to fill up any containers with the last of the water in the pipes. *But maybe Jenny had a few more crayons to Puck's half-empty box.*

"Almost out. Mama Dee had some jugs, but Jenny drinks a lot of water."

Guess not.

"Come on, then. This is a good time to show you how to get water from a well."

Grayson went into the barn and came back with a cylinder-shaped tube, a handful of tools, and a thick coil of rope wrapped around his shoulder. The silver cylinder was three and half inches in diameter and 52 inches long. It was made from galvanized stove pipe by an Amish man.

"Is that a rocket?" Puck asked with big, hopeful eyes.

"No. It's an Amish water bucket. Anyone can use this on nearly any well and get fresh drinking water. You don't have to boil it or treat it. Straight from Mother Earth."

"That doesn't look like a bucket. It's too skinny."

"That's because nowadays, wells are thin." Grayson turned the bucket upside down and held it out to Puck. "See here, this end has a rubber valve fastened to a shaft that runs the full length of the bucket. It opens to let water enter the bucket, and then it closes when the bucket is lifted."

Puck looked thoroughly confused. Grayson was used to that. He'd received the same look when he'd shown the bucket to Olivia. When people thought about wells and buckets, they typically imagined what they'd seen on television on old shows like *Lassie*; stone wells that were waist-high, set up off the ground, around a deep hole with a bucket tied to a rope and crank.

Those were a thing of the past.

"Come on, I'll show you how it works." As he walked to the back yard, he kept talking, "I bought this one online from Lehman's, but you could make your own out of PVC pipe, if you could figure out how to do the valve on the bottom. It was less than a hundred bucks, so not worth the headache for me. And anyone could do this, even my wife, Olivia. It's simple."

Well, maybe not Olivia, but he'd bet her sister, Gabby, could figure it out. Olivia would think it was too hard and probably wouldn't even try, unless he made her.

"You could also use a hand pump to get water out of your well much faster than this bucket. This one only pulls up two gallons at a time. A hand pump would be much more efficient. But I can't find mine. Luckily, I have this, too."

As they walked, he stole a glance at Puck to be sure he was paying attention; he may as well try to teach the boy something if he was going to hang around. "Well it wasn't actually luck, Puck. See, when you prepare for emergencies, one is none and two is one."

Now Puck looked even *more* thoroughly confused; if that was possible.

"What I mean is, if I hadn't prepared with two different plans to get water out of my well, I wouldn't be able to get any. Because apparently, someone *stole* my hand pump which was my number one plan," he said angrily.

"Wasn't me."

Grayson laughed. "I know it wasn't you. You've never even been here before I found you in that tree and brought you home."

Puck stopped walking and dropped his head, looking at the ground, still as a statue.

"What are you doing?" It was as though someone had pulled his plug. Grayson stopped to wait up for him. "Come on, Puck."

Puck didn't move.

Grayson walked back to him. "What's the matter, boy?"

Puck took a deep breath and spoke, without looking at Grayson. "I was here, Mister Gray Man. I took those veggies from your garden, for Jenny."

Grayson stared at the kid long and hard, ready to give him a piece of his mind.

The boy began to tremble.

"Hey, hey... don't. Don't do that."

He put his hand on Puck's shoulder and Puck flinched and backed up.

Shocked by his response, Grayson stepped back and dropped his hand. Someone had been mean to this kid, and Grayson couldn't stand to see the boy so full of fear. "Whoa. I'm not gonna hit you. *Ever*. It's okay. But listen, Puck. If you really need something, you need to *ask* first. There's nothing on this earth worse than a thief or a liar. *Or* a murderer. You hear me? Just don't do it again."

"I'm sorry." Puck stuck his lip out and let his head hang.

"S'kay. Let's get this project going."

Grayson walked on ahead just as Ozzie ran over and dropped his ball at Puck's feet. That changed his mood in an instant. As though it'd never happened, he laughed and grabbed the ball, throwing it far enough to earn a home run. Out of the park—or backyard anyway.

Would've made a great baseball player.

Ozzie took off to retrieve it and Puck caught up with Grayson just after he'd tipped over the old fake doghouse that covered the well-head and pulled the well-cap off. Then he pulled out the drop-pipe that housed the submersible pump motor, handing the end of it to Puck and telling him to walk it back as he pulled.

"What is it?"

"It's what the well-pump is attached to. It doesn't work without power, but when it does, the pump shoots the water through this drop-pipe. We have to take it out so that we can get our bucket down to the water in the actual well."

He came to the end of the pipe, and gently pulled out his pump, hoping it wouldn't give him any trouble if the power came back on and he had to re-install it. He laid that aside and picked up the well-bucket, running his rope through the large metal ring on the top and tying a tight knot.

He handed it to Puck.

"Okay, now you just carefully feed this well-bucket into the well. When it gets to the water, it'll stop dropping so easily, and you'll want to wait a minute or so to let it fill up, then pull it back out, and *boom*... we'll have fresh, clean drinking water."

Puck was excited to help. He carefully took the well bucket from Grayson and inserted it into the well, looking down his nose with big eyes at the dark hole into which he was dropping it.

"That's it, lower it down easy..." Grayson instructed him.

The pile of rope on the ground was getting smaller and smaller. Grayson had no idea how much rope he actually had, but so far, the hole had eaten a good bit of it. A smarter man would've stretched the rope out beside the drop-pipe he'd just pulled out to see if he had enough to reach the water *before* attempting it.

Too late for that.

Puck was working *very* slowly, dropping it inch by inch. He'd told the boy to go easy, but this was killing him. He stood up and put his hands on his back, leaning backward to stretch just as Ozzie came flying in with his ball, dropping it at Puck's feet.

Delighted, Puck let go of the rope and grabbed the ball, throwing it again.

Grayson lunged and missed, landing in the grass with his fingers clutching at air. He threw himself to his feet and cussed up a storm as he watched the end of his rope disappear deep into the dark chasm.

"We're back to one is none, Puck."

GABBY BOLTED UPRIGHT in the bed; a strange bed. She gaped around at the unfamiliar room.

Two twin beds, one of which she was in, were covered in tattered but comfy quilts. A simple four-drawer dresser sat between the beds, holding a huge white pitcher next to a matching over-sized bowl. A stack of wash clothes and a tiny tower of Dixie paper cups were neatly stacked beside the oversized water pitcher.

A hand-made tapestry on the wall quoted *The Lord's Prayer*, hanging directly over a messy pile of pillows and blankets on the carpeted floor, big enough to accommodate two. Her backpack leaned against the corner, next to Olivia's beat-up, duct-taped flip-flops.

Remembering where they were, and that they were safe, Gabby dropped back down on a flattened feather pillow in relief. In the bed opposite her, Mei turned over and slowly forced her blood-red eyes open. She stared at

Gabby, blinking several times, and then gave up and closed them again, rolling over to face the wall.

Gabby jumped out of bed. "Get up, Mei. We've got to go. We're going to make it home today. Where's Olivia and Emma?" she asked while pulling on her sneakers. She peeked into the pitcher to find it full of water, but she wasn't interested in drinking it yet. They'd had their fill last night when Elmer, the farmer, had brought them home and now, she needed to empty her bladder.

She also needed to do *the other*. She'd stuffed herself when Edith, the farmer's wife, had happily prepared a late supper for the girls. Cold chicken, cheese, sliced tomatoes and cucumber salad had been ready and waiting for them when they'd walked into the cozy home.

"Don't know," Mei muttered.

Gabby poured some water into the bowl and used a washcloth to rinse off her face and hands. She turned and shook Mei's shoulder gently. "Come on, if you're going with us, you need to get up. You've got five minutes." Standing over her, Gabby could see trails of mascara dried on Mei's cheeks.

She, Olivia and Emma had fallen asleep nearly the second their heads hit the pillows, but apparently Mei had been awake at least part of the night. Those tear trails hadn't been there when they'd gone to bed. She wondered if the tears were because of the little girl in the picture. She couldn't blame her for that, but they all missed their loved ones. She missed her husband, Jake. Olivia missed her own husband, Grayson, and her step-daughter, Graysie. And

Emma especially could feel Mei's pain. Emma had hardly made a peep about her husband, Dusty, and her son, Rickey. It was sort of unspoken between the three of them that they wouldn't whine and cry over their families. Instead, they'd focus on just getting back to them.

Gabby opened the bedroom door to the aroma of bacon cooking. Sighing in appreciation, she followed her nose to the kitchen, which was just a few feet away in the small farmhouse. Edith stood at the counter in a brightly-flowered muumuu dress and pink bunny slippers, sliding homemade biscuits off a flat pan and onto a plate. An antique wood stove held a percolating pot of coffee. Gabby's mouth watered.

"Good morning, Edith, where do I...um... use the bathroom?"

Edith's silver hair was piled in a large flat bun atop her head. She turned and smiled. "Good morning, honey. It's the second door down the hall."

She wasn't sure if she was expecting Edith to point her outside or what. She had no idea how far outside of town they were and didn't want to assume they were on their own well and septic tank. "Does the toilet work?"

Edith nodded. "Yes, of course. When you're finished doing your business, just pour water into the tank. You'll see a green line inside where the waterline has set for years. Just fill it up to there. After you flush, pour a bit into the bowl for the next person, if you don't mind."

Gabby stepped into the bathroom to find it ready for use. Five buckets stood lined up against the wall, some full and some only half full. The shower curtain was pulled back from the claw-footed tub and it was still wet. Her sisters had probably taken a spot-bath.

She too would love to clean all her lady parts, but she was up late. They needed to get on the road. She could relax in a bath at the homestead, maybe even today. She did her business and flushed and then did as Edith asked, making sure the toilet bowl had water in it too.

Another station with soap and a towel was set up in the bathroom on top of a low antique apothecary, this time with only two metal bowls, for washing and rinsing, and a Tupperware pitcher full of water. She washed her hands and went back to the kitchen, clearing her throat to alert Edith she was behind her. She didn't want to startle her.

Edith turned and greeted her once more with a smile. "You look well-rested. Your sisters beat you out of bed. They're outside with Elmer."

Gabby smiled back at the adorable little woman, wondering if this is what their mother would have looked like if she'd lived to see her golden years.

She accepted a cup of coffee and took the first sip, sighing in pleasure. "Thank you so much...for everything."

Elmer had been a god-send; sent by Edith, of course. The old couple took them in, fed them, and listened to them re-hash their story—leaving out the part about how they found Mei— before Edith tucked them all in for the night, assuring them they were safe and kissing them good-night as though they were little girls. Even Mei had stoically accepted her affections.

They were good people, even if Elmer *tried* to come across as cantankerous and put-out.

Edith waved off her thanks with a red-checked gingham dishtowel and began cutting bacon into biscuit-sized strips. She sliced each butter-topped biscuit in half and loaded them down with the bacon, delicately arranging them on a napkin-covered plate.

Gabby stepped to the screen door and looked out, once again, nearly not believing her eyes.

Emma and Olivia were out in the pasture with Elmer, all three walking in a robotic fashion, dragging their feet—Olivia's feet wearing a pair of the loudest Nike sneakers in fluorescent pink and orange that Gabby had ever seen—and walking back and forth, sliding past each other as though they were magnetically attached to the grass.

"What are they doing?" Gabby asked.

"Gathering dew for drinking. We've got plenty of water, but Elmer doesn't want you girls out there on the road again not knowing how to get some if you need it." She handed Gabby a buttered bacon biscuit. "Here, you can have one, but call your sisters in to breakfast for me."

Gabby cupped the biscuit to her face, inhaling the smell of melted butter, fresh baked bread and bacon. "Thank you, again." Edith nodded and gently pat Gabby's back. "You're welcome, dear."

The screen door squeaked as Gabby stepped out.

She walked over to the pasture, waiting to call them for breakfast until she could get a closer look at what they were doing. She nearly laughed when she was close enough to see both of her sisters trailing blue shammy towels—like they used to dry their cars—tied around their ankles. They scooted through the tall grass like little energizer bunnies with their brows furrowed and elbows bent.

Even funnier was that Elmer was doing it too, dressed in the same overalls and John Deere cap that he'd worn the night before, dragging his boots with his head down and back bent.

She laughed and he looked up. "'Bout time you got up, your sisters here are doing all the work." He waved Olivia and Emma to him and together they walked toward Gabby, passing her to get to the four metal water bottles lined up on the stoop.

Emma and Olivia squatted down to untie their shammy towels and proudly held them out to Elmer, who wrung each one, squeezing and twisting the morning dew out over the open water bottles. With the water from his own towels, he was able to top them off.

"Wow." Gabby nodded in approval, wondering how many passes that had taken. "Can we drink it just like that? It's safe?"

He handed each of them a bottle and held onto the fourth. "Of course it's safe. It's *dew*. Straight from God." He looked around. "Where's your friend?"

"She's not up yet. I'll go in and roust her again," Gabby answered.

"Your sisters' told me where you found her."

So her story was out too. Gabby was embarrassed for

her. She looked to her sisters, who refused to meet her eyes. *Gossipers.*

Elmer clicked his tongue in sympathy. "That's a sad thing. Y'all did good getting her away from those men. But that girl's in bad shape. I could see that last night." Elmer put one foot on the stoop and his hands on his hips. He chewed the inside of his mouth while he thought for a moment. "I'm not sure she'll make it the rest of the way. I figure you girls have about another day—and maybe more —of walking before you're scraping the welcome mat."

Olivia shrugged. "I think she'll feel better when she gets up. We were all tired and dehydrated last night. I feel a ton better." She tapped her god-awful sneakers together. "See what Edith gave me?" she asked Gabby.

Gabby nodded. "Nice," she lied.

Elmer sniffed loudly. "It's not about being tired. That girl is a junkie. She's was hurting last night and it's only going to get worse. It'll could take a month to get drugs out of her system. It looks like she's only been without a few days."

Olivia looked at him in confusion.

Gabby cocked her head. "Yeah? What makes you think so?"

Elmer chewed the side of his mouth again. Then he turned and gave them his back. The pause was so long, Gabby was beginning to think he wasn't going to answer. Finally, he turned around. "I've seen it up close and personal, just like that. I lost my boy to that mess. She's scratching, and muttering. Probably confused. Paranoid.

And she's still in bed, so she's already feeling it suck her energy away. You can't trust her. I learned that the hard way. She'll beg, borrow and sell her own mother to get that stuff back into her system. Best y'all part ways soon... not here. But somewhere before you get home."

"We can't just *leave* her," Olivia said indignantly. "She's all alone, and she only has *one hand*. And she's hurt. I told you, Elmer. They *branded* her like...like... a cow. We have to help her."

Gabby looked from Olivia to Elmer, praying he'd have wise words to convince her sister otherwise. Mei had been setting off her alarms since they'd rescued her—if that *was* indeed a rescue—and Gabby agreed with Elmer; it was time to cut her loose. People on drugs brought nothing but trouble. *Not my circus; not my monkeys.*

Elmer squinted his eyes and gave Olivia his full attention. "This ain't about her physical disabilities. It's about her *mental* state. You can't help people like that. They won't listen to you. The demons in their heads talk louder. And if the power doesn't come back on, they'll be in the first wave."

"What wave?" Olivia asked.

"The first wave of people to kick the bucket. Anyone on drugs, whether they have a doctor script or not, is going to be hurting." He looked over his shoulder at Edith working in the kitchen and lowered his voice. "Elderly people and drug addicts *both* are going to die. When my heart and blood pressure pills are gone, I won't last long myself. But I'll go quick. People like your friend though, they're going to suffer mighty badly. And there ain't no clinics open to help them. They'll be wishing for death within a week. Like I said, I watched it with my son. Me and Edith suffered along with him. And you'll be suffering too, if she goes home with you."

Elmer swiped at an eye and cleared his throat. "I wouldn't wish that kind of suffering on anyone." He turned suddenly and stepped into the house, leaving Gabby, Olivia and Emma alone.

Gabby and Emma both squeezed Olivia's hands. She stood stone-still with watery eyes.

"I agree, Olivia. We should have seen the signs. They're all there now that he mentioned it," said Gabby. She looked to Emma for support.

"Me, too. I knew there was something wrong with that girl," Emma said, nodding.

Olivia shook her head. "I'm not leaving her."

Gabby knew there was no use trying to talk Olivia into it. Once she had broken free from her first husband who'd physically abused her, she'd dedicated her life to helping other woman in bad situations. Man problems, drug problems, job problems. Didn't matter. Olivia wouldn't turn one away. It was admirable, but sometimes Olivia needed to put herself and her family first. This was one of those times.

Gabby shrugged. "I know you want to help her, but I won't let her put any of us in jeopardy. I think she's trouble, and if she gives us a hassle, she's gone. I've got one goal, and that's to get us home safe and sound with no more drama on the way."

*M*ei stood shaking beside the open bedroom window, with her back against the wall. She waited until the girls had stepped into the kitchen before quietly pulling the window down.

She'd known all along they were talking about her behind her back. Now, she'd caught them. She had barely slept a wink last night, and no one really cared, other than the one ditzy sister. She'd listened to their steady breathing all night, envying their peaceful slumber. Envying their lives. They had each other. And they had *husbands*.

Elmer and Edith had each other, too.

She had nobody.

And no one cared.

But by the time she was through, they'd *all* care. And in the end, maybe she'd finally get a good night's sleep, too.

She awkwardly dug through Gabby's bag. Frustrated, she cussed to herself. She couldn't find what she was looking for. But that was okay. She'd find a way to make them pay...

26

BRIGHT LIGHT POURED through the window, waking Jake.

One eye squinted open.

He was home. *Alone.* Gabby still not here.

After his run-in with the thugs at the shop, Jake had changed his mind about coming home. He just wanted to get somewhere safe. Home was closer than Grayson's so he'd made a bee-line back to the neighborhood, and shut off the 4-wheeler at the entrance, quietly pushing it down the street and into his garage.

He hadn't wanted to deal with the neighbors again. He'd had enough stress.

Slowly, he pulled himself out of bed, his head and body aching. Time to get on the road before someone discovered he was home. Especially Tucker. He might want his four-wheeler back after all.

And for all Jake knew, his wife might be sitting at Grayson's right now wondering where the heck he was.

He'd actually hoped she *was* there. He'd gladly take a chewing-out from Gabby, if only he could see her today.

He opened the refrigerator and then quickly slammed it shut, cursing his laziness. Something stunk. Gabby would probably kill him over not throwing away all the food or cooking what could be saved. He hadn't done a thing since the power went out. It wasn't like him.

He cursed the demon on his back, grabbed a Gatorade and ate a bowl of dry cereal, and then he hit the road. Grayson would have plenty of food later.

---

*L*oose rocks spun through the air as Jake slid the four-wheeler to a sudden stop on the dirt road. He'd heard a woman scream. He looked over his shoulder at the woman standing in the middle of the road waving at him; she must've stepped out of the woods as he passed by. He backed the ATV up and turned it around, and sped back to her.

"Hi," the woman said in a friendly voice. "I saw your hat. It matches mine." She pointed to her head. "See."

The woman wore an exact replica of Gabby's favorite hat, with the TSS Logo; she also wore a pistol in clear view, holstered to her side. He watched her carefully but her hand didn't hover anywhere near it.

"You're with The Shooting Sisterhood?" he asked, in confusion.

"Yeah, like what are the chances of that, huh?" she

answered and laughed. "My friend and I were here for a shooting competition. Power went out. No gas to get home. We're sort of stuck."

The shooting range was on the way here, although he hadn't passed it himself. He'd taken a short cut to get this far.

Jake took his hat off and looked at it to be sure. Perfect match. "This is actually my wife's hat. Her name is Gabby."

"Gabby is your wife? I know her! Well, from our group on Facebook. We chat sometimes. We were hoping to meet her in person while we were here but we didn't see her at the shoot. My name's Tina."

"We?

"Yeah, I have another friend with me. She's in there." The woman pointed her thumb toward the trees.

"What are y'all doing out here?"

She shrugged. "Camping out. What else? The only motel we could find in this area was a hole in the wall. Toilets were overflowing. People were getting upset. We don't know another soul there, so we headed out of town limits to be safer—get away from the crazies. Been camping here for a few days now."

Jake thought about it. The odds of running into two of Gabby's friends, on the way to Grayson's house, during an apocalyptic event such as this were probably a million to one. But he did know the motel she was speaking of, it was the only hotel near them in York County without walking a very long way, and she was right. It was a rat hole even before the power went out.

But the paranoid side of Jake wondered if Gabby had mentioned the homestead as a bug-out location to her. Women who liked to shoot were more times than not also preppers, and it could've come up in a private conversation. Maybe they'd set up camp here on purpose, hoping to run into Gabby.

"What's your plan?" he asked suspiciously.

Tina threw her hands up in the air. "To get home. But we have to wait for the power to come back on or find some gas. What else? Don't have much choice," she said and laughed.

Jake raised an eyebrow. For a woman, she didn't seem all that panicked about being stuck away from home, squatting in the woods. This wasn't passing his smell test. Grayson had always warned about *The Golden Horde*; people who hadn't prepared that would eventually come creeping out of the chaos of town into the country; people who'd do anything to get to your food and supplies if the shit ever hit the fan.

Tina watched him carefully and laughed again. "Look, cowboy. We're not looking for a knight in shining armor. We both have one of those at home and we intend to get back to them. I was going to quietly watch you go by like I have a dozen other people, but I saw the hat. That's all. Thought it was weird and before I realized it I called out. You can get back on your way." She stepped out onto the road and held a hand out. "Tell Gabby that Tina and Tarra say hi."

Jake took her hand and slowly shook it, looking into her

face for any sign of duplicity. He saw none. Now that he thought she might *not* want his help, he couldn't just ride away without seeing if they were okay, even though she looked healthy enough. Actually, more than that. She was attractive with her long hair and cat-shaped eyes. She wore a tight black T-Shirt, emphasizing strong arms, and camo pants covering a shape that would definitely turn heads. She wasn't dirty or desperate at all.

A woman like this shouldn't be stranded far from her *knight in shining armor*, as she put it.

"You ladies have food and water?" he asked.

Tina gave him an almost patronizing smile and nodded. "Yeah, we've got plenty."

How could they have plenty if they'd walked here and been camping for days? Surely any food they'd had with them—and water—would be gone by now. Jake wasn't aware of a river or creek anywhere near. Maybe that was her pride talking?

His conscious pricked at him. What if Gabby and the girls needed help right now wherever they were stranded? He'd been hoping and praying for days that someone would step up and help them, if and when they needed it. He'd be a hypocrite to not do something for these women now.

"Can I meet your friend?" he asked, hoping to get a look at their campsite and see how they were faring before making any decisions.

"Sure. Come on." She tilted her head toward the woods.

"Here's a wide enough opening to get your 4-wheeler through."

Jake waited for her to get out of the way, and then drove the ATV through the ditch, and just into the edge of the woods, hiding it from view. He got off and followed as Tina quietly stalked through the woods, admiring her skills. She barely rustled a leaf, quiet as a mouse.

He sounded like a herd of elephants as he walked.

They approached the campsite from behind, and he saw the other woman, Tarra, who was doing something that nearly blew Jake's mind. She had a small piece of wood tapped into a tree, and under that she was tying an empty water bottle to the trunk, held tightly to the tree with a boot shoelace.

In just a moment, he watched in astonishment as clean, clear water began to drip into the bottle.

"How'd you do that?" he asked, startling the woman, who reacted by whipping around and reaching for her own pistol, quick as lightning.

Jake flinched. These women were no shrinking violets.

Before she pulled the gun free, Tina stepped in front of Jake. "Wait, Tarra. This is Gabby's husband. He's okay."

It took Tarra a moment before her face fell into a friendly smile and Jake studied her. Strong chin and clear hazel eyes, she wore a ReelCamo Girl tank top with tight blue jeans and boots. The headband she wore with her bouncy pony-tail was also ReelCamoGirl. Jake recognized the brand, as he'd been forced to look through pictures of women on Facebook wearing it when Gabby decided she wanted some for her birthday. She looked clean enough to have just finished a photo session. She also didn't look as though she needed his help.

These women couldn't hold a candle to his Gabby, but they were both attractive women; too cute to be out on their own in a strange town living in the woods. Grayson might get mad, but Gabby would never forgive him if he just left them here.

And he was more afraid of Gabby then Grayson; by a long shot.

Jake tried to make friends with Tarra, feeling terrible for catching her off guard. "Can you show me how to do that? Is it a special tree or something?"

Tarra laughed. "They're all special trees. Most of them are good for something. This one is a Birch. They're everywhere in this area. Plenty of water. Just have to make sure you don't drain too much from one tree and that you cover the hole. Otherwise, you'd kill the tree."

"That's so cool. I want to learn how to do that."

"Google it. There's tons of YouTube videos that show you how," Tarra answered, and then laughed, letting him know she was kidding—sort of.

"Tarra," Tina admonished her. "She's kidding. It's easy to do. First, you need a Sycamore, a Birch or a Hickory Tree. Then you just find a small stick to use as a spout—or a tap —you'll need to carve it down to flatten it on each end so the water runs smoothly off of it.

Then find a flat spot on your tree and angle your knife up and give it a firm smack to imbed the tip of the knife into it about two centimeters. Give it a little wiggle. If you did it right, you'll see water right away running down the knife. Then you drive your tap up into the hole with the flattened end you made, making sure it's pointed down. Keep messing with it until the sap rolls down the stick instead of the trunk of the tree and position a container under it. It takes about an hour to get a full bottle, but works every time. Just be sure to cover the hole really well when you're done or you'll kill the tree, like Tarra said. You can even get sugar sap from Maple trees this same way if you need a sugar spike, or if you want some pancake syrup."

Jake nodded. "Impressive. I'll have to try that."

He looked around at their campsite. They'd built a solid lean-to against a large fallen tree and covered it with layers of full branches, still green, and even plugged the holes with moss. It looked cozy enough. From the opening, he could see two good sleeping bags stretched out with travel pillows and pads underneath. Between their beds, there was a small sawed-off log being used as a table. A lantern sat on the table beside a solar charger, not being used at the moment, with an emergency hand-crank radio/flashlight combo.

"You picking up anything on the radio?" he asked.

"Not yet," Tina answered. "Maybe soon, though. We keep trying."

Outside their lean-to shelter, they'd built a nice camp-fire ring with stones. One side had a make-shift rock oven of sorts. The other side held two racks made of sticks between two forked branches. On one of the racks a small pot of soup hung, bubbling, and on the other side a rabbit was slowly browning. It smelled delicious and Jake's mouth watered. Stacked on a nearby log they were using as a table were camp-plates, two spork combos and actual condiments; salt, pepper, and Texas Pete. A half dozen more bottles of water were lined up next to it.

Tina stepped up and expertly turned the rabbit on the spit.

A sizable stack of firewood lay cut and split, all ready for burning, and an axe leaned beside it. The campsite was neat, functional and cozy. He looked around in awe.

Definitely not shrinking violets. He was impressed. Maybe they didn't need his help after all? Heck, maybe he and Grayson needed *their* help.

He took a deep breath and gave it another thought. The least he could do was offer. "I'm headed to my brother-in-law's homestead down the road a piece. Y'all are welcome to follow me there if you want."

Tarra and Tina exchanged serious looks.

Jake hurried to answer their unasked question. "Gabby and her sisters are hopefully on their way. They were on a beach trip when the lights went out. They might even be there now."

"Who else is there?" Tarra asked suspiciously.

Jake held his hands up, palms out. "I don't know for sure, but I assume just my brother-in-law, Grayson. He's married to Gabby's twin sister, Olivia. He's harmless. We both are," he finished, followed with a nervous laugh.

"We've got plenty of food and water there. You two can hold up until we figure out a way to get you home, if you want."

Tina and Tarra exchanged another look with each other and then looked around their camp. They were unfazed. They had what they needed right here, obviously.

Tarra shrugged. "We've got plenty of food and water, too. We actually eat pretty well between the small game and the vegetation out here. We can get bigger game if we need it. I got that rabbit today, but yesterday Tina trapped two squirrels and we had squirrels and gravy for dinner. We're not going hungry. But a bath would be nice."

Tina laughed at her friend and then nodded. "Agree. A bit more company would be cool too—and we'd both love to meet Gabby. How about you draw us a map, and we'll talk about it between ourselves. Maybe we'll head that way. Maybe we won't. But we really do appreciate the offer."

Jake nodded, relieved. "Sounds good. It's no more than an hour's walk. I'll write it down if you have some paper."

Tina crawled into the lean-to and grabbed a huge back-pack, and conveniently pulled out a pen and notebook.

Of course she did.

Jake took a few moments to map it out and then shook both of their hands, promising to give their regards to Gabby, if they didn't show up themselves to say hello. He wished them well and hurried back to his ATV, in a hurry to get to Grayson's—as well as to get out of the woods alone with two pretty women...just in case his wife should happen that way all of a sudden.

Crazy times and all that...

He noisily forced his way back through the woods, feeling like a bull in a China shop. When he saw the road, he expected to see his 4-wheeler. Somehow, he must've got turned around.

It wasn't there.

He turned in a circle. Behind him, he could just barely see the women deeper in the woods. He was in the right place...

Stepping out of the woods into the road, he looked first one way, and then the other, just in time to see his—actually, *not* his—4-wheeler hauling ass and kicking up dirt behind it as the thief high-tailed it out of there. Tucker wasn't going to be happy with him.

"Damn it!" he yelled, taking Gabby's hat off and slapping his leg. He couldn't care less about the 4-wheeler, but he and Gabby's wedding picture was in his bag. And they took that, too.

Tina and Tarra jogged out to find Jake stalking up and down the road, swarping and swearing at his loss. They gave him his space and talked quietly until he noticed them.

Jake faced them with a red face, still spitting mad. "Took my damn bag. My stuff. My water. *My gun*. And me and Gabby's wedding picture for fucks sake!"

"You didn't have your gun *on* you?" Tina asked in amazement.

"No! I hate guns. Damn thing isn't even loaded."

He stomped off and paced back and forth another minute and then turned back to the women and took in a deep breath. He held it for a moment and then apologized. "I'm sorry about my language, ladies. I'll be heading out now."

He turned to walk away.

The women whispered to each other, and Tarra spoke up. "Wait. Give us time to break up camp. We'll walk with you."

"You're coming with me?" Jake asked, confused.

Tina shrugged. "Not much choice now. You showed that thief where our camp was. He'll be back for more, probably sneaking in tonight after it gets dark. We don't plan to be here when he does. And you...well, *someone* needs to watch your six."

MEI WATCHED AS GABBY, Olivia and Emma all lined up for training by Elmer. He was teaching them how to shoot a shotgun, while she sat on the porch step watching them closely. He insisted the girls take the gun with them, just in case. They were going to finish shooting, and then get on the road, hoping to be home by nightfall.

More walking...

She couldn't take it anymore though. They wouldn't all be leaving here.

She'd let them have their peaceful breakfast, and she'd eaten her fill and then some. Why not? She was hungry. But the repeated blast of the shotgun had her nerves jumping. She sat with her hand and her stump over her ears, flinching each time the gun roared.

Gabby and Olivia had handled the shotgun without a hitch, both shooting toward the stack of hay that Elmer had attached a huge target to. The target was now scraps of paper, blowing in the wind and the hay had a large hole blasted in it. It was Olivia's turn. Mei almost felt sorry for her.

Almost.

It was clear that Olivia's twin sister, Gabby, was head and shoulders above her twin in nearly every way. She was stronger, braver, smarter, not as whiney, and knew how to survive in the woods without a man—or at least she did okay as long as she had the bug-out bag, as Gabby ridiculously kept calling it. And her husband had packed that. However, she had to give full credit to Gabby for getting her out of the clutches of the motorcycle gang and getting them this far.

But had Gabby really done her a favor? Maybe she would have been better off trading her body for food and water and at least having someone take care of her. After hearing the girls talking earlier, she knew she wouldn't have a home with them. She couldn't fight the demons inside of her. These women would eventually throw her away, just as everyone else in her life had done.

It wasn't fair. Why should they all be blessed, and not her? She wasn't always like this. She could be either one of them. A mother. A wife. A sister.

But she wasn't.

Not anymore.

She'd always drawn the short straw in life.

It's time to even up the straws.

She watched as Gabby stood shoulder to shoulder with Emma, encouraging Olivia to just give it a try. She had her hip cocked out, thinking she was all that. The pistol she hoarded and lorded over them stuck out from the waistband of her shapely pants. *A real Annie Oakley there*, she thought. Gabby acted as though it didn't bother her at all it was back there.

Maybe it should've.

"Come on, now girl. You can do this," Elmer grunted. He was getting irritated. "Your sisters did it. They're still alive and kicking."

Olivia stuck her hands in her pockets and smiled shyly. "We already have a gun, Elmer. And Gabby knows how to shoot it. We don't need another one. *I* don't need to shoot," she insisted.

Elmer snorted. "Can't depend on your sister to get you out of every scrap. What if someone takes her gun? Come on up here. You're stronger than you think you are."

Gabby took Olivia's hand and dragged her forward a few steps. "He's right, Olivia. Anything could happen out there. Emma and I will trade off carrying the shotty," she winked at Elmer, having adopted his nickname for the gun. "You only need to know how to shoot it in case of an emergency."

Mei rolled her eyes at Gabby. Clearly, Olivia didn't want to. Why was it okay to force her sister to do something she didn't want to do?

Olivia adamantly refused. *Good for her.*

Elmer caught Mei's eye. "How 'bout you? Want to learn to shoot it?"

"No," Mei answered.

Elmer gave her a stern look. "Why not? Step up here, I'll show you how."

Gabby ran a hand over her face and turned her back to Mei, and said something. It was clear she didn't want Mei to hear what she was saying, but Mei wasn't stupid. Either Gabby didn't trust her, or she thought she couldn't shoot with one hand.

She was wrong.

Mei stood up, fire boiling in her veins. She wasn't a bad person. She was just like Gabby, except she'd made the mistake of trusting her doctor. Two years ago, she'd been normal. A botched abortion and an even worse hysterectomy had led her to pain pills—pills that she was legally prescribed. She'd had no idea they'd trap her in a never-ending cycle of grief and need and more pain. When she couldn't get the prescriptions anymore, she'd been left alone to deal with the withdrawals.

To relieve her pain, she'd turned to other drugs that she could find out on the street.

Then they took her little girl from her and she had more pain—more pain needed more drugs.

When she ran out of money, she'd stolen drugs—a lot of drugs—from the wrong person.

She'd paid heavily for that, and ended up with only one hand.

And then, she'd never stolen again. But she kept paying with what was left of her body.

And her soul.

She *had* to feed the need.

And now she was here.

But that didn't mean Gabby was any better than she was.

She bit down on her lip and stomped over as though she were going to take a lesson from Elmer, but walked past him straight to Gabby, who still had her back turned to her.

Mei jerked the pistol from the back of her pants and jumped back, holding it in the air with her one shaky hand.

Gabby gasped and whipped around. "What are you doing?"

Emma put her hands up and stepped back.

"Young lady, put that gun down!" Elmer roared, stepping toward Mei.

Mei pointed the gun at him. "Stop. I'll shoot."

"What in tarnation's going on with ya? Have you done lost your mind?" he yelled. He tore his hat off his head and slapped his leg with it. Tufts of his cottony-white hair danced in the wind.

Olivia stood frozen. Emma stood still and silent, her hands in the air beginning to shake.

Gabby stood defiant, not stepping back or holding her hands up.

Mei waved the pistol, pointing it at Gabby, then back again at Elmer. "Maybe I have lost my mind. If I have, it's your fault.

All of you. People just like you. You all think you're so much *better* than me. I heard you talking. I listened to you sleep so soundly. I *see* you. But no one sees me. No one knows my pain. No one cares," Mei screamed at them, tears running down her face. "I had a *daughter*. I was a mother. I was a good person, too."

Olivia took a step forward, "You *are* a good person. Of course you are! We know that."

"Stop," Mei screamed, whipping the gun around to point at Olivia. "You don't know. You know nothing!" Her skinny arm shook in an effort to keep the gun up. Hot tears streamed down her face.

Olivia visibly cringed and backed up another step.

"Put that damn gun down, girl," Elmer yelled. "Before you hurt someone."

Mei turned the gun on him again. He stood stock still. "There's only one person I want to hurt." Then she waved it around to aim at Gabby. Her finger moved into the trigger-guard as the gun shook violently. She stared at Gabby with hatred in her eyes, and firmed her jaw.

"No," Emma screamed while Olivia dropped to her knees with her hands up and begged, "Please. Please don't shoot her," she said. She clenched her hands together as though in prayer while her knees sunk into the soft ground.

Gabby took another step toward Mei, watching her carefully. "Get up, Olivia. You and Emma go into the house. Hurry."

"No! I'm not leaving you!" she yelled at Gabby, and looked to Mei. "Listen to me. We *saved* you. Gabby saved you. Please don't do this," Olivia begged through tears. "We'll help you, I promise."

"There's no help for me."

Before anyone could answer she squeezed the trigger.

Time stood still as the bullet ripped through the air, silencing everyone and everything as it cut through flesh and bone, sending a spray of crimson out the backside of the beautiful, dark hair.

28

GRAYSIE SLAPPED at the air in front of her. After piling into yet another heap of hay in yet another empty barn stall, and gorging on a bag of GORP, washed down with a bottle of water, she'd meant to close her eyes for just a moment.

But she'd fallen asleep—again.

The night before, after the excitement of her escape from the university and the ensuing car wreck had finally caught up with her, her adrenaline had fizzled out, replaced with exhaustion. She'd drifted off on her side with one arm draped through her backpack and her gun still stuck in the waistband of the back of her pants. She'd slept for hours, and got up and walked for hours more, lost in the dark. Turned out the country roads and barns all looked the same at night. She hadn't been anywhere near her dad's house.

When the sun finally showed its face this morning, she'd sat down with her map and tried to figure out where she was. It was hopeless. It all looked like squiggly lines to her and some asshat had taken down all the street signs—if there'd ever been any.

Midday, she'd stumbled onto another empty barn and laid down for a quick nap. She'd overslept... and now the bugs wouldn't leave her alone, buzzing around her face and ears.

She waved her hand in front of her nose again and pulled herself up into a sitting position, not remembering where she was for a moment.

She opened her eyes.

Moonlight shone through the spaces where boards were missing from the barn—how did it get to be night again? She'd slept *that* long?

She pushed herself up and screamed.

Squatted beside her, a man stared at her with buggy eyes that darted all around. Nearly buried within a baggy, stained sweatshirt, with shaggy hair and a scabbed up skeletal face, he leered at her with a crooked smile of gaping holes and rotten teeth. He reached for her bag, his arm covered in a network of collapsed veins and scabs.

His hands shook violently. "Hey, 'lil red riding hood. You got anything to us get geared up?"

His breath was deadly. She cringed. "Geared up? No! You can't have my stuff." Graysie grabbed her bag and scooted back, and jumped to her feet. She felt for her gun. It was still in the back of her pants, surprisingly.

He scrambled unsteadily to his feet, too, startled by her scream.

He held his hands up, palms out, on too-skinny arms. "Yo, sorry. No, I don't want your gear. Look, I didn't mean to scare you. I just...need to *go fast*, ya know? Get *scattered*, man."

"No! Get away from me." Graysie stared at his once-youthful, but now prematurely-gaunt face with disgust and quickly looked around the barn as she hooked her arms into her backpack and slid it into place onto her shoulders. She was cornered in the stall. Her only escape was to crawl over the side, but with the heavy backpack, he'd be on her in a second.

His face changed, becoming angry. He lunged at Graysie with his scab-covered arms, grabbing a handful of her curly red hair. "I know you've got someth—"

She could hear her father's words whispering in her ear dozens of times as he'd wrestled with her, or pushed her around in horse-play... *fight like a man, Graysie. Don't let me win...*

She stepped into his lunge and grabbed his wrist. His eyes widened in a stunned daze as she slammed the palm of her other hand into his elbow, bending it the wrong way. She felt a *snap*. He stumbled away, with an ear-piercing shriek and clutched his arm. She prayed it was broken as she turned and raced out of the barn, without looking back at the screaming demon behind her.

29

THE LADIES

HOURS LATER, Olivia tossed a flower—provided by Edith—onto the mound of dirt and sank to her knees once again. She covered her face, hiding the dirt and tears, as she rocked back and forth and sobbed. She wept with a force that nearly choked her.

Emma stood between Elmer and Edith, looking small beneath Edith's arm around her slim shoulders that shook with grief. She did her best to be strong, but watching her sister cry broke her. She couldn't hold it back; she bawled too, and Elmer quietly patted her back. The old couple sang Amazing Grace quietly, barely in a whisper as they too swiped tears from their faces.

"Well, that's that, then," Elmer said gruffly, once they ended their song. "Get up, Olivia. I'm taking you and your sisters home." He walked away toward his barn while Olivia and Emma turned to watch him in confusion.

They hurried after him, stepping into the barn just

behind him to find Gabby stacking hay bales onto a wagon that was attached to a John Deere tractor. The hay was stacked high into the air in a perfect square. She bent and grabbed a pile of old quilts and moved to the end of the wagon, stepping up and disappearing.

Olivia sniffed and wiped her nose on her balled-up Kleenex. "What are you doing, Gabby?"

Gabby didn't answer. She was still mad as fire at Mei. Mad that she couldn't stop her. Mad that they'd found out too late the pain she was in and the loss of her daughter she'd been going through. Mad that their country didn't realize their own doctors had started an epidemic of drug addiction before it was too late. She *hated* drugs. In her darkest days many years ago, she too had nearly given up and lost her life to a handful of prescription drugs.

She fought back her own grief with wrath as she angrily swung one bale after another to the top row, nearly finishing it off.

"She's building you a fort," Elmer answered for her. "I figure you girls are only about an hour from home, the way the crow flies. May as well take you home myself and make sure you all get there." He dropped his head and stared at his boots. "I don't want any more blood on my hands."

Olivia put an arm around the old man and squeezed. She looked up at him. "It wasn't your fault, Elmer. It wasn't even your gun."

"Well, I'm taking you anyway," he grumbled. He gently shook off her one-armed hug and made himself busy checking to be sure the trailer was securely attached to the tractor. Then he grabbed the heavy gas containers that were stacked against the wall and grunting with exertion, he handed them up to Gabby one at a time, and she dragged them inside their hay-fort.

He stood back and nodded his head. "Good job, Gabby. Now y'all girls go say your goodbyes to the missus. We leave in five minutes."

Emma scratched her head. "If you have gas, why not just drive us in your truck?"

"I don't have gas. The tractor runs on diesel. I have that. Besides, this tractor can push pert'near anything out of the way. We don't know if the roads are clear between here and there, and even if we did have gas, we don't know that my old truck would make it anyway. I don't trust it like I do my tractor," he muttered, and walked away, patting the tractor on the hood affectionately as he walked by it.

Gabby, Olivia and Emma ran into the house, gathered their things, and stood still while Edith fussed over them, handing them each a brown bag packed with food and two gallons of sweet tea. She sniffled and wiped at her nose with a fancy handkerchief while she gave them teary goodbyes.

Outside the window, they watched as Elmer pulled the tractor out of the barn and into the backyard. They stepped outside, and Elmer jumped down. He stood still and leaned over for a peck on the cheek from his wife, promised her he'd be safely home tomorrow and stoically climbed up into the seat without another word.

One more hug from Edith, and they climbed up into the

hay, Gabby last. She stacked three bales in the space they'd clambered through and yelled *giddy-up* to Elmer, before dropping down between her sisters and putting her arms around them. Gabby looked at her sister's hands and then her own. They all matched, covered in dirt and dotted with blisters from the rough handles of the shovels.

They all huddled up and leaned in close, drawing strength from each other to beat down the gruesome memory of Mei lying dead in a puddle of blood with her long black hair in a halo around her. And Mei laying in a hole in the ground with her arms crossed over her thin chest, the picture of the pig-tailed little girl tucked beneath them and a silly bandana tied around her head. And Mei's face as it disappeared under a cascade of dirt, peaceful, and finally free from her suffering.

Each of them thought about what they'd been through on their girl-trip.

Worst vacation ever.

But finally, it was over, and soon they thought, they'd all be safe at last; away from all this madness.

—But they couldn't be more wrong.

30

GRAYSON

OZZIE WHINED and scratched at the bedroom door. Grayson mumbled and fumbled out of the bed, finally giving up on sleep and giving in to him.

Damn it, it's past midnight.

He'd be glad when Olivia was home to take care of them; he'd had no idea how exhausting it was to spend the day letting the dog out, then letting the dog in, then letting the dog out, then letting the dog in...

Guilt pinched his conscience as he realized he was making a fuss over nothing. The dog had needs. And he loved the hairy beast anyway. He'd kept Grayson sane while he'd been alone with his worry over his family. It wasn't Ozzie's fault that Grayson had never got around to putting in a doggy-door. That was going on his honey-do list as soon as the world righted itself. They'd all benefit from that. Besides, he couldn't sleep worth a damn for the worry picking at his brain.

"Come on then, Oz." He patted the dog on his way out the bedroom door.

Suddenly, he remembered Jake was there.

He could barely believe it. Finally, he and Ozzie weren't alone anymore. He tried to push away the selfish thought that he'd rather have his brother there instead. Jake's arrival had been dampened with the bad news he was carrying about Dusty and Rickey.

Shocking news.

News he wasn't looking forward to telling Emma.

But at least Jake would be here to share that burden. Grayson was glad to see him. He was family too, even if not by blood. And he was damn handy to have around. Hopefully Jake was just the first to arrive, and soon he'd hold his wife and daughter again. Wherever the girls were sleeping tonight, he prayed they were all safe and comfortable and that come daybreak, they'd be coming down the driveway, right into his arms.

And hopefully their wives wouldn't freak out over the fact there were half-naked women sleeping across the hall *—wait, hopefully they weren't half-naked.* He needed to get his mind right...

Grayson stumbled through the dark house as quietly as he could and opened the front door, stepping out onto the porch. Ozzie ran down the steps to do his business while Grayson stepped up to the side railing and did the same, yawning and stretching while he watered the flowers— thinking that was the only thing he could appreciate about

Olivia being gone; he could pee outside without her nagging at him.

She didn't understand that he was also marking his territory, just like Ozzie. Some animals would shy away from human urine, so she was keeping him from doing his *duty* as man of the house when she insisted he use the bathroom. He could hear her now... *'Grayson, I can't believe you walked right past two toilets just to pee outside! You're going to kill my flowers!'*

He looked up at the moon and howled quietly while he peed.

Then, he gave it a shake and chuckled. *She'll never know.*

"—Hi, Mr. Gray Man," a voice rang out of the darkness like a shot.

"Son of a *gun*, Puck!" Grayson jumped and nearly fell off the porch trying to pull his pants up and turn away from Puck—who was up in a tree—at the same time.

Puck shimmied down the tree, fast as a monkey, and dropped into a crouch to rub Ozzie.

Grayson took a deep breath and slowly let it out. "You startled me, boy. Don't you know it ain't polite to sneak up on a man at the butt crack of midnight?"

Puck giggled. "You said butt-crack."

Grayson ran his hands through his hair, and a muscle jumped in his jaw, reminding his tooth to scream in pain. "What are you doing up there?"

The smile disappeared from Puck's face. "I came to see Ozzie. Are you mad?"

Ozzie ran to the porch and grabbed his ball and came

back, sliding in and dropping it at Puck's feet, slobberingly delirious to see the kid. Puck snatched it up, apparently forgetting he was in the middle of a conversation. Grayson noticed he was limping as he ran away with the dog in pursuit.

He looked at the dark sky and gave a silent prayer; a plea for patience to deal with Puck without losing his temper and scaring the kid again, and then he muttered in an exaggeratedly-polite tone to himself—practicing, "Why yes, Puck, I *am* annoyed. I don't especially like to show off my pecker to just anyone, you see. I'd much rather have dinner and a movie first, if I had my rather."

The screen door slamming on his way back into the house punctuated his sarcasm the way his quiet voice couldn't. Now that Ozzie had woken him, and Puck was here, it was going to be awhile before he could go back to sleep. He'd just lay awake and worry about Olivia and Graysie if he tried. May as well sit up a spell.

Time for coffee.

*T*wenty minutes later Grayson sat beside his brother-in-law, Jake, on the porch, sipping on a cup of java. He gave silent thanks for the Coleman camp stove *and* his percolator. At least some things were still quick and easy, and he had plenty of fuel for it.

The smell of coffee—with a side of worry and a slam of the screen door—had dragged Jake out of bed too. He said he wasn't able to sleep anyway. Grayson was sure the same thoughts were keeping them both up.

When Jake had arrived earlier, with two women in tow, Grayson had wanted to punch him in the face *and* hug him at the same time.

After a brief shouting match about where he'd been and who'd been responsible for letting the gas go bad—and it damn well *was* Jake's fault—they'd stumbled together for a very non-manly hug crowned with damp eyes.

Now they sat in near-silence, other than the crickets and cicadas, and Grayson wanted to fill it with words— words with a grown-up. *Finally.* Not a full-grown kid or a dog.

He really wanted to hash out the what-if's about the women and Graysie again, but he knew he and Jake would come to the same conclusion. There were at least a half dozen ways to get to and from the beach. The chance they'd find the girls on the road was slim to none, and they didn't have enough gas to try all the different routes; not even close.

He couldn't help still being a bit angry with Jake about the gas he'd let go bad.

Better to talk about something else.

He searched his thoughts for something—anything. But with no news, no visitors other than Puck, and no way to watch TV, he had nothing. His only thoughts were on their family or the *event* that turned out the lights, and what it might be.

Or Trixler.

He could talk about the mysteries of Trixler all day. After reluctantly voting for the outrageously non-political Trixler, just to do his part to keep Hillary out of office, he was shocked to actually see the man keeping his promises and getting things done. If people could look past his unpolished rhetoric, immature tweets and personal attacks on his own staff and the media, he was surprisingly doing a good job. If he continued to keep his campaign promises, could he really make America better—against all odds?

Grayson could argue the fact that welfare hand-outs were down, illegal immigration was down. Jobs were up. The country was a trillion dollars richer in the first year of his presidency. But with no social media, who was left to argue with?

Not Jake.

Good ole salt-of-the-earth Jake would maintain a neutral status on anything and everything to avoid conflict.

In black and white, good things *were* happening with the country. Numbers didn't lie. If only Trixler would stop setting twitter-fires and picking fights so that the rest of America could see it. But the way things were going, they couldn't see past the fire, much of it flamed by the main-stream media.

However, with the lights going out, all of it might have been for naught. Who knew who had done this? How would they ever find out with communications down?

"So, Jake, what do you really think happened? What's going on? Who did this? Russia? Maybe *for* North Korea?

Or China... they've always been a big helpful brother to the Norks."

Jake shrugged. "Still don't know, man."

Grayson eyeballed Jake.

He knew full well Jake didn't like to talk politics. When it came to choosing sides, Jake was Switzerland. He'd need to be careful where the conversation went. "So, you don't think this has anything to do with Trixler pissing in Kim's Cheerios?"

Jake shrugged again.

Okay, North Korea is off limits. *Unless maybe I soften him up with a joke first.* "So, if this all ends up being some pissing contest between us and North Korea—and other adversaries took their side, things could get really bad." He gave Jake a very serious look.

Jake nodded.

"No, seriously, man. Just imagine Trixler and Kim *together*. Do you know what you get when you cross a penis and a potato?"

Jake smirked. *Finally* showing some life. "What?"

"A dicktator!" Grayson laughed loudly at his own joke and Jake spared him a chuckle, but then laughed louder at Grayson's unusual silliness and his willingness to poke fun at Trixler, seeing as Grayson had coaxed the whole family into voting for the man—in solidarity against what happened at Benghazi with the other candidate. They'd cast their votes against her in support of the military, and law enforcement, too, which she'd had no respect for during her campaign.

Trixler, on the other hand, supported the military and the boys in blue.

"Wait!" Grayson said. "You know what led to this? Everyone in America is suddenly *offended* about everything. When the parties became too divisive, we started making mistakes. We shouldn't even call this a *nation* anymore. You know what you call a country where everyone is pissed off?"

Jake raised his eyebrow and tilted his head.

"A Urination," Grayson blurted out loudly. He slapped his knee and guffawed loudly, amusing Jake and getting another smile from him.

Puck ran by, chasing fireflies as Ozzie pranced around him, both of them blissfully happy. They took off together around the back of the house, disappearing from sight, but not before Grayson noticed the limp seemed to be worse the longer Puck ran around. Earlier the kid had told them Jenny had kicked him. That made Grayson feel a little bit better about the girl. If she could kick that hard...

As though he could read Grayson's thoughts, Jake nodded his head toward the direction Puck had gone. "That kid is something else."

Grayson nodded and smiled. The boy was growing on him.

"How old is he?" Jake asked.

"He said eighteen or nineteen, I forget which. Hard to remember he's that old when he acts like an overgrown child."

Jake cleared his throat. "So, you think he's safe to be around the women, and Graysie?"

Grayson gave it a moment's thought before answering, "I'd say so. He seems pretty harmless. But he's not going to stay here. He's got a home, and he's got Jenny there to keep him company."

"That's the reason I asked you. I didn't want to mention this earlier in front of anyone, but he's got a young woman over there that's *not* his sister, or family, and she's around his age, and he mentioned to me he liked to touch her hair, so it sounds like he's sweet on her. You'd think she'd be meeting his er...*needs*."

Grayson rubbed his jaw. His sore tooth was starting up again. In the excitement of Jake arriving, he'd forgotten it. Or maybe the pain had dulled, but it was roaring now. "I'm not sure he has those kinds of needs. He's really like a kid— in a man's body. He might not be playing with a full deck, but he doesn't have a mean bone in his body. And he's still an innocent. I think kissing is about as far as he'd go. He probably has no idea there *is* anything further than that."

"I don't know about that," Jake answered. "When we came up the road today, I saw him first, before he saw me. He was sitting against a tree at the edge of your property." Jake stopped, covering his embarrassment with a half-smile. "He had his britches down."

Grayson shrugged. "Maybe he was taking a shit?"

Jake shook his head. "No, man. He was beating that thing like it owed him money."

Grayson wrinkled his nose and cringed. "Oh *no*. I

could've lived without that scene in my head. Seriously? In my yard?"

He and Jake both laughed out loud, but really, it worried Grayson. Maybe that girl—Jenny—wasn't so safe there after all. Puck might be child-like in his head, but physically, he was a *big* man. Having urges and not understanding them could be dangerous. It might be best if Jenny came over and stayed with them, especially now they had other women here, until Puck's mama came home.

Still, he hadn't made an attempt to meet her yet, and Puck hadn't offered to introduce him. He'd need to move that up as a priority; maybe in the morning.

Jake cocked his head. "Did you hear that?"

"I heard something. Maybe an owl?" Grayson answered.

"Ozzie," Puck yelled from behind the house. "Ozzie!"

Jake and Grayson stood up and ran off the porch, and around the house, just in time to see Ozzie take off like a bat out of hell through the field behind the house, with Puck following behind.

"Grab your gun, Grayson! I'll follow them," Jake yelled as he took off in pursuit.

31

GRAYSIE RAN like the hounds of hell were after her. The branches slapped at her without mercy. Briars and brambles left her cut and bleeding. Water streamed from the corner of her eyes and splattered back to wet her face. She sprinted, adrenaline feeding energy to her tired limbs. She darted faster and faster through the trees, barely feeling her feet on the ground.

There!

She could see a break in the tree line and caught a glimpse of a pasture as she dashed closer and closer, finally seeing the outline of a farmhouse beyond it—dark and squatting—the windows black except for the moonlight reflecting off them, giving the house a threatening, sinister appearance, as if it lay in wait for Graysie to reach it.

But that farmhouse was far less threatening than the woods.

Moonlight peeped in as she raced on, and the bigger

trees mimicked the shadow of a man, jumping out to frighten her over and over again; she didn't know if he was chasing her or if it was her imagination fueled by terror.

Panting with effort, she pushed on almost to the edge where the woods would finally release her into the field. She stopped for a moment, sucking in air and feeling a little bit of relief.

But it was short-lived.

Before she could step out into the field, the forest exploded all around her.

She stumbled in the dark. Her feet tangled beneath her and she crashed down toward the forest floor. She squeezed her eyes tight as she fell, realizing he'd won the game. *He was right behind me the whole time. Now the son of a bitch has me.* She twisted her body before she hit the ground, trying to land on her back.

She'd still fight.

She'd fight like a man, just like her daddy had taught her.

Just before her head hit the ground, she opened her eyes and saw him; a dark blur barreling toward her—

GRAYSIE STRUGGLED to pull her pistol out from behind her as time slowed. The dark blur flew at her and she screamed, just before the shape of a man emerged and collided with the blur—Ozzie!—in the same split second she pulled her pistol free, pulled back the hammer and squeezed the trigger.

The gun loudly boomed, barking death.

The blur twisted in the air and barreled toward Graysie.

Man and dog went down in tangled heap.

Graysie scrambled to her feet at the same time as Ozzie, who crawled out from under the man's arm and nearly flew to her, almost knocking her back over with his enthusiasm.

Filled with terror at what she'd done, she dropped the gun with a little toss, as if it were too hot to hold. She rubbed Ozzie's head with both hands, checking to be sure he wasn't hit. "You okay, boy?"

Ozzie was fine, barely winded even. She realized the

farmhouse she'd seen from the back was her dad's house. She was a lot closer than she'd thought coming in the back way.

The man on the ground moaned and Ozzie ran back to him, nudging at his leg.

Graysie stepped closer and pulled Ozzie away by his collar. "Watch out, Ozzie!" With the limited moonlight, Graysie couldn't see much of his face, but he didn't look like a tweaker. He was huge. Healthy.

Not like the sick guy in the barn. But the fact was he was out in the middle of the night, on her dad's property, chasing either Ozzie, or her. She'd never seen him before. He had to be with the other guy.

"Who are you? Were you chasing my dog?" she yelled at him, fear making her voice shake. "What's your name?"

The man hesitated and then moaned, "Fuuuucking Pu —" his words broke off as he screamed in pain through clenched teeth. He grabbed his wound. Blood seeped through his fingers.

Like a cold shower, anger replaced Graysie's fear for a moment. He was trying to hurt Ozzie? What kind of freak would hurt a dog, especially a sweet dog like Ozzie? She had to be sure that's what he was saying. "What?"

The man didn't answer. He moaned and tried to roll over.

A different kind of fear knotted inside her. *What if he dies? Am I in trouble?* But if he was with the guy who attacked her, it was self-defense. Graysie yelled at him, "Look, were you with the meth head in the barn?"

He answered with a whimper.

The fear in his voice made Graysie feel stronger. She nudged him with her foot. "Who are you? Were you chasing me, or Ozzie?"

"*Fucking* Pu—" he yelled through clamped teeth, breaking off again with a sob, not able to speak through the agony.

"Stop cussing my dog!" Graysie screamed at him.

Ozzie stepped up to him again and sniffed, and then buried his nose in the man's side, pushing at him. Graysie pulled on the dog's collar, bringing him to a safe distance. He jerked free again, running back to the man and licked his face. He whined.

"Ozzie, leave him alone. He can't hurt us anymore." Graysie reached for Ozzie again, and to her shock and surprise, the man twisted and rolled to his stomach, and struggled on the ground.

He was trying to get up.

She jumped forward and grabbed Ozzie's collar, forcefully pulling him away from the man. She had to get away. She had to run.

Gripping the collar, she frantically looked for her bag and her gun, both hidden in the darkness on the ground. She whipped around to check the man again. He was on all fours now, wobbling and moaning. His blood puddled beneath him. He fell back to the ground again, but continued to struggle.

A glint of moonlight reflected off the gun. She snatched it up and took off, abandoning her bag, pulling at Ozzie

with all her might. She cut to the side of the field that met
the road, hoping to draw the creep away from her father's
house, in case he was able to get up. If she could make it to
the other side of the road, they could disappear into those
woods and quietly circle back to her dad's.

Finally, Ozzie stopped resisting and ran with her. He
loped easily beside her frantic leaps through the field. Her
heart beat rapidly, hammering in her chest. The tweaker
was still out there too. He could pop up any minute.

She threw a glance over her shoulder, hoping not to see
the bloody man behind her. No sign of him yet. She pushed
harder, and felt a stitch in her side. Her blood pumped
loudly in her ears; that's all she could hear. It was as though
all other sound ceased.

Digging deeper, she pumped her arms back and forth
as she pushed through the discomfort. Finally, the dirt road
appeared through a thin stand of trees, just across a ditch.

Not breaking her stride, she ripped through the trees
and jumped the ditch, seeing Ozzie slide to a halt out of the
corner of her eye as she leapt. Too late to stop, she went
airborne and landed on the dirt road, skidding in bits of
tiny gravel on her knees...directly in front of a screaming
monster hiding behind two blinding beams of light bearing
down on her. A cloud of red dirt followed it as it barreled
down the road growling toward her.

Her bloodcurdling scream rang through the air as she
hunkered down on her knees, holding her arms over her
head, just as she heard her father's voice in her head calling
out for her in a scream that matched her own.

Finally, the monster came to an abrupt stop, inches from Graysie as she knelt, head-down between the glaring twin beams. A moment later, the monster was silenced.

She held still a moment, still not daring to believe she was still alive, and then turned her head and tried to peek through her fingers at her newest foe.

"Graysie!"

She whipped her face the other way toward the familiar voice—it wasn't in her head after all—and nearly fainted with relief to see her dad running down the road, with her Uncle Jake right behind him.

Grayson slid in the dirt, gathering his daughter in his arms. "Graysie, are you okay?" he breathlessly asked, as he hugged her.

"Dad!" She clung to him, her head against his chest, willing it to be true. She was home? This was real? She wasn't dead? "I'm okay...but there's a—"

"Grayson!" a voice yelled above them.

The both looked up to the astonished face of Olivia, Emma, Gabby, and an old man, all standing over them, lit up by a tractor's lights.

Grayson scrambled to his feet and pulled his wife to him with one arm, and dragged Graysie up with the other, pulling them both in and squeezing them to his pounding heart. "You're home? You're *both* home?"

Olivia joyously laughed through her tears and nodded.

"You're home!" he said again, this time believing his eyes. The cold knot he'd carried in his stomach for days on end finally loosened, and tears pricked at his eyes, and then ran unchecked down his cheeks.

He turned to see Gabby run to Jake as Olivia finally let loose with a stream of chatter, spilling the goriest details of their journey to her husband in such a rush that she couldn't be understood. He smiled down at her and waited for her to take a breath.

"*J*ake!" Gabby screamed.

Jake jogged as fast as he could with his bum leg, eating up the space between them. They flew together with enough force to nearly knock them down. Jake threw his arms around his wife and twirled her through the air. "I knew you'd make it!"

Gabby laughed, trying to choke back her cries. "It wasn't easy. It was a rough trip," she said, her voice breaking. She pulled him in tighter and held her breath, trying to keep the tears in.

Jake hugged her harder. "You're okay now. I've got you."

Gabby turned to see Olivia chattering while Grayson looked down at his daughter in confusion, trying to hear what she was saying, as she and his wife both competed for his attention. "Dad, there's a ma—"

The night erupted in voices all going at once, and Ozzie jumped up on Olivia's leg to get her attention. She fell backward onto the road and the dog jumped on her chest as she fought to keep his kisses off her face.

Grayson pulled away from Graysie's grasp. "Just a minute, sweetie." He reached down to pull Ozzie away from Olivia and held a hand out to his wife, pulling her back up. The dog barked loudly and happily and ran in silly circles around them, ducking and diving with his tail in the air, overjoyed to see his mistress, and seemingly over the moon to have his family all together again.

Olivia cooed and chattered to her dog as he ran around her. "I missed you too..."

Jake squinted his eyes at the light and yelled over the dog barking to Gabby, "Who's that man at the tractor with Emma?"

Grayson fought back tears as he watched Ozzie run circles around their little family, together again, and then he looked around, suddenly remembering what had brought him out here. "Where's Puck?" he asked out loud, mostly to himself, knowing the dog couldn't answer him.

Graysie again yelled something, her words lost in the chaos as everyone ignored her.

Elmer pulled his hat off and scratched his head at the chaos around him. It brought a smile to his old mug, until he noticed Emma standing alone, a tear rolling down her face.

He and Edith had enjoyed hearing all about Emma's husband, Dusty, and her son, Rickey.

So, where were they?

He stepped over and pulled Emma to him, giving her a one-armed hug, sheltering her beneath his strong arm as she sadly looked around in confusion. "Where's Dusty and Rickey?" she finally yelled over the ruckus to Grayson.

That caught Grayson's attention. He gently pulled away from Graysie, ignoring her chatter, and swiped a hand over his face, feeling terrible for ignoring his little brother's bride. He didn't want to be the bearer of bad news right here and now, but she deserved an answer as she stood sad and alone. "Dusty and Rickey are—"

Graysie stuck two fingers in her mouth and whistled, piercing the air just the way her dad had taught her to do if she ever needed him. She had their attention now.

"Hey! *Listen* to me," she shouted.

The crowd silenced and Graysie erupted in a flurry of words. "There was a man... in a barn, not far from here. He attacked me and chased me. I hurt him. Maybe broke his arm—no, wait. He wasn't the one chasing me. There was another man. *He* came after me." She paused and took a breath, then shook her head in frustration.

She looked around in confusion and saw Ozzie. "There were *two* men. I lost one at the barn. The other one came at Ozzie. Or maybe Ozzie attacked him. I don't know."

Grayson grabbed her shoulders and looked down at his daughter, examining her from head to toe. "Where are they now? Did they... hurt you, Graysie?"

She shook her head. "No. I fought him. Just like you taught me." Her voice broke, and her teeth chattered. Shock was setting in. "I g-g-got away."

She dropped her head to stare at her feet, not able to

look her father in the eyes. Her shoulders sagged and her body tremored and then shook like a leaf.

Everyone watched silently as Graysie fell apart. Grayson squeezed her shoulders. He looked firmly into her eyes. "It's okay. *You're* okay. You did well. I'm proud of you."

Graysie tried to shake off his hands, but he didn't budge. "N-n-no. You d-d-don't understand. I... I d-d-did something terrible. The second man... O-O-Ozzie was trying to s-s-save me from him. And he cussed him. He cussed our dog... called him a *f-f-fucking pup*, so I kicked him when he was down." Her hands shook as she reached behind her and pulled out her father's gun. She carefully handed it to him, stock first. "But before that...I didn't just fight back, Dad. I sh..sh..shot him. I *shot* a man," she finished and then collapsed in his arms.

Grayson held his daughter and looked at Jake in shock. Jake stared back with wide eyes. "Are you sure he said fucking *pup*?"

*T*hat's all, folks. Book One had to end somewhere... we're past 300 page in print now! I hope you'll keep reading the series.

Also, sign up here to be notified when each book is available: http://eepurl.com/bMDLT1

ALSO BY L.L. AKERS

Keep reading The SHTF Series; the attack that took down the grid was just the beginning...

Book 1: *Fight Like a Man*

Book 2: *Shoot Like a Girl*

Book 3: *Run Like the Wind*

Book 4: *Wait Like a Stone*

Want to read the origin stories of the SHTF characters? While it's a different genre (not post-apoc), this psychological suspense 4-

book series described as 'dark, but beautiful,' will take you back to the *Very Beginning* of the three sisters and later, when they met their partners. It will introduce you to Grayson, the MC of The SHTF Series and explain *why* he became a Prepper:

The *Let Me Go Series*.

What have the bloggers said about The Let Me Go Series?

★★★★★ "Breathtakingly beautiful." -*Not Everyone's Mama Book Blog*

★★★★★ "I was mind blown. The ending of the book was absolutely perfect." -*MetInEleven.blogspot.sg/*

★★★★★ "There's no way *Let Me Go* can be excused as a typical NA book... I absolutely love this type of book." -*ReadingIsMyTreasure.Blogspot.com*

★★★★★ "Riveting and gut-wrenching, a captivating

read. Full of emotion." *-BookwormBrandee.blogspot.ca*

★★★★★ "An emotional journey not to be missed." *-BooksLiveForever.com*

★★★★★ "Every word of this book begs attention, every sentence squeezing out emotion." *-MySeryniti.com*

★★★★★ "A gripping tale... This book packs quite a punch." *-BookyThoughtsAndMe.com*

★★★★★ "A rollercoaster of emotions." *-Adventures In Reading*

★★★★★ "L.L. Akers' book is a well-written and emotional book." *-Bibliobelles.com*

A Heart for War

A novella (short story): previously published in the full
novel nominated for Audio of the Year 2020: Archie's
Heart (no longer available in print/ebook).

*When China occupies the United States in a coordinated
attack, one bitter, lone veteran with his dog, Shithead, must
choose whether to bug-out alone, or find his heart amidst a
group of teenagers hoping to bring honor back to a dead soldier
and liberate their country in this emotional post-apocalyptic
war story.*

For L.L. Akers full catalog, and to hit the "FOLLOW" button to be notified by Amazon via email when new publications are released, please click FOLLOW.

AFTERWORD

In determining what sort of event this series would focus on, research led the author to a recent conclusion by the Federal Bureau of Investigation's (FBI) that states cyber-attacks are eclipsing terrorism as the primary threat facing the United States.

If nothing else, the author hopes that anyone still on the fence about the need to 'prepare,' will do their own research, and realize the threat of cyber-attacks, EMP's and/or natural disasters are more than fodder for fictional conspiracy and/or disaster novels. The threats are real. The danger is imminent. The need to prep and prepare in order to protect your family is essential. Even if it's not a national event, look at Puerto Rico...Texas...Florida. A little bit of prepping would go a long way in case of a localized natural disaster, too.

Also, please note, there are many characters in this series, from both sides of the political divide. Don't assume

Afterword

any one character speaks for the author. They are each different (fictional) people, with their own thoughts and beliefs—some you may agree with—some you may not; but it'd be a rather boring story if everyone held the same opinions.

ABOUT THE AUTHOR

L.L. Akers is a prepper, located in the Carolinas, who enjoys marksmanship shooting, canning fruits and veggies, riding ATV's and studying potential survival situations with eyes wide open, and head out of the sand.

Sign up to the Shit (hit the fan) List if you want to be notified via email when the next book comes out.

Also, find out what I'm reading. Click the pic!

www.llakersbooks.com
contactllakers@gmail.com

Printed in Great Britain
by Amazon

61716882R00182